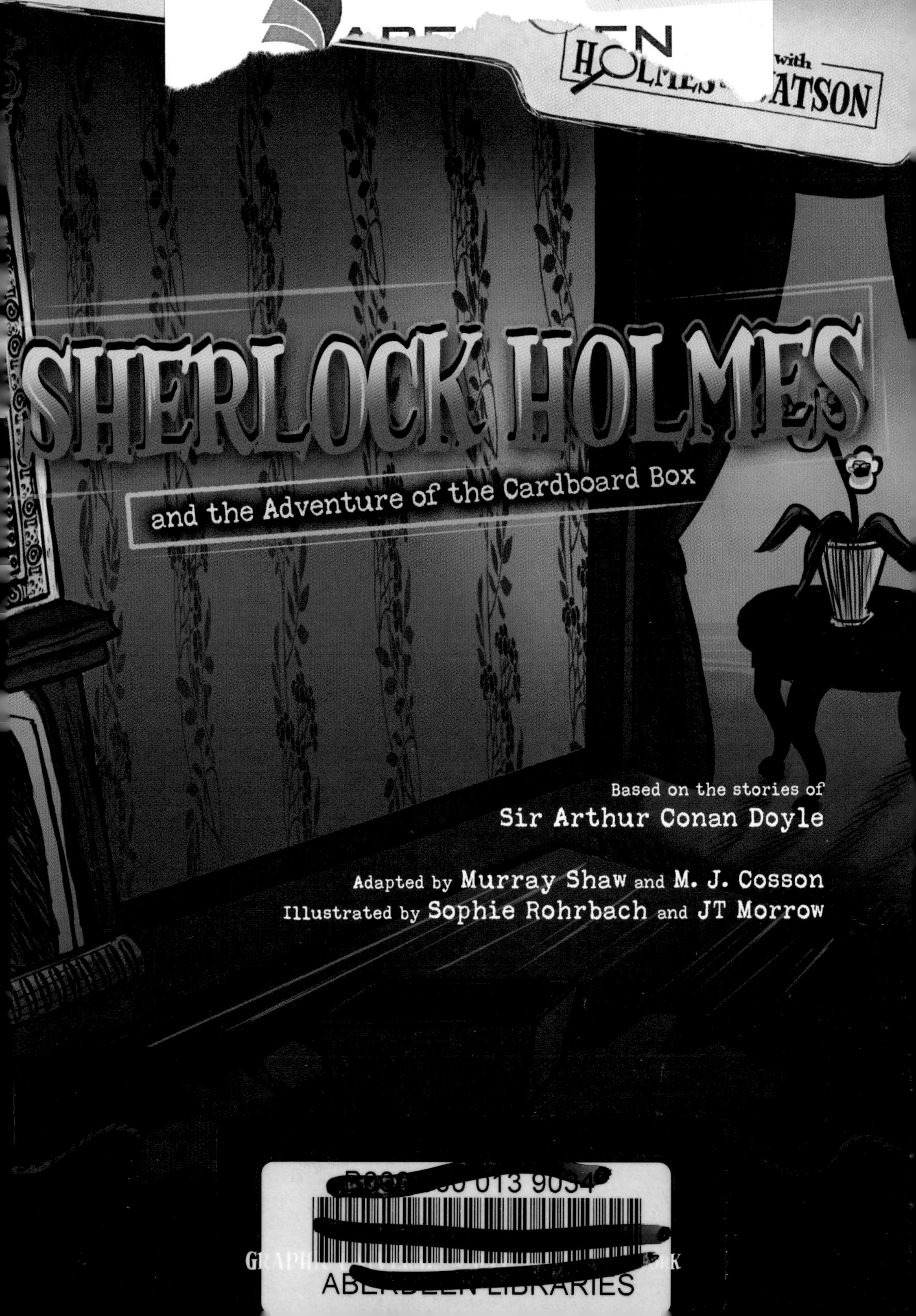

SHERLOCK HOLMES

and the Adventure of the Cardboard Box

Based on the stories of
Sir Arthur Conan Doyle

Adapted by Murray Shaw and M. J. Cosson
Illustrated by Sophie Rohrbach and JT Morrow

Grateful acknowledgment to Dame Jean Conan Doyle for permission to use the
Sherlock Holmes characters created by Sir Arthur Conan Doyle

Text copyright © 2012 by Murray Shaw
Illustrations © 2012 by Lerner Publishing Group, Inc.

Graphic Universe™ is a trademark of Lerner Publishing Group, Inc.

Graphic Universe™
A division of Lerner Publishing Group, Inc.
241 First Avenue North
Minneapolis, MN 55401 U.S.A.

Website address: www.lernerbooks.com

Shaw, Murray.
    Sherlock Holmes and the adventure of the cardboard box / based on the
stories of Sir Arthur Conan Doyle ; adapted by Murray Shaw and M. J. Cosson ;
illustrated by Sophie Rohrbach and JT Morrow.
    p.   cm. — (On the case with Holmes and Watson ; #12)
    Summary: Retold in graphic novel form, Sherlock Holmes investigates when a
spinster receives a package in the mail containing two severed ears. Includes
a section explaining Holmes's reasoning and the clues he used to solve the
mystery.
    ISBN: 978-0-7613-7090-1 (lib. bdg. : alk. paper)
    1. Graphic novels. (1. Graphic novels. 2. Doyle, Arthur Conan, Sir, 1859-
1930. Adventure of the cardboard box—Adaptations. 3. Mystery and detective
stories.) I. Cosson, M. J. II. Rohrbach, Sophie, ill. III. Morrow, JT, ill. IV.
Doyle, Arthur Conan, Sir, 1859-1930. Adventure of the cardboard box. V. Title.
PZ7.7.S46Shh 2012
741.5'973—dc22   2011005113

Manufactured in the United States of America
1—BC—12/31/11

The Story of
SHERLOCK HOLMES
the Famous Detective

Sherlock Holmes and his helpful friend Dr. John Watson are fictional characters created by British writer Sir Arthur Conan Doyle. Doyle published his first novel about the pair, *A Study in Scarlet*, in 1887, and it became very successful. Doyle went on to write fifty-six short stories, as well as three more novels about Holmes's adventures—*The Sign of Four* (1890), *The Hound of the Baskervilles* (1902), and *The Valley of Fear* (1915).

Sherlock Holmes and Dr. Watson have become some of the most famous book characters of all time. Holmes spent most of his time solving mysteries, but he also had a wide array of hobbies, such as playing the violin, boxing, and sword fighting. Watson, a retired army doctor, met Holmes through a mutual friend when Holmes was looking for a roommate. Watson lived with Holmes for several years at 221B Baker Street before marrying and moving out. However, after his marriage, Watson continued to assist Holmes with his cases.

The original versions of the Sherlock Holmes stories are still printed, and many have been made into movies and television shows. Readers continue to be impressed by Holmes's detective methods of observation and scientific reason.

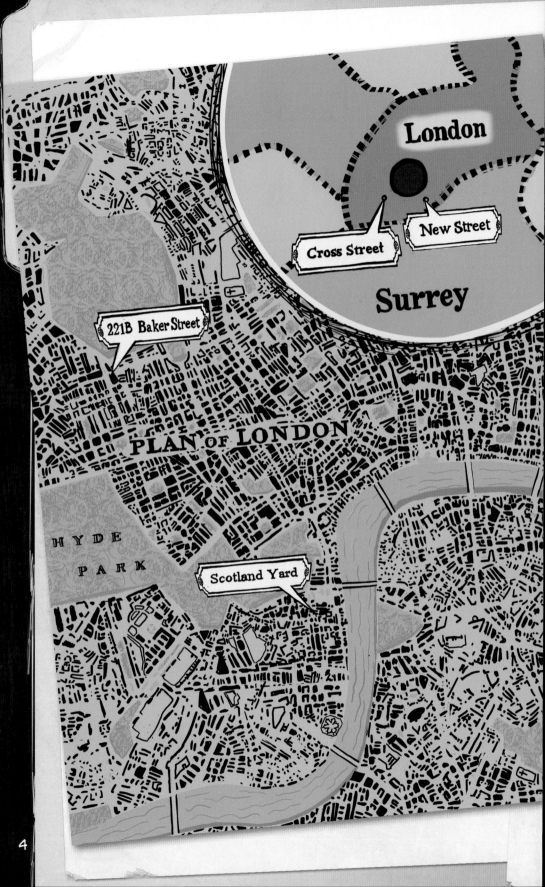

London

Cross Street

New Street

Surrey

221B Baker Street

PLAN OF LONDON

HYDE

PARK

Scotland Yard

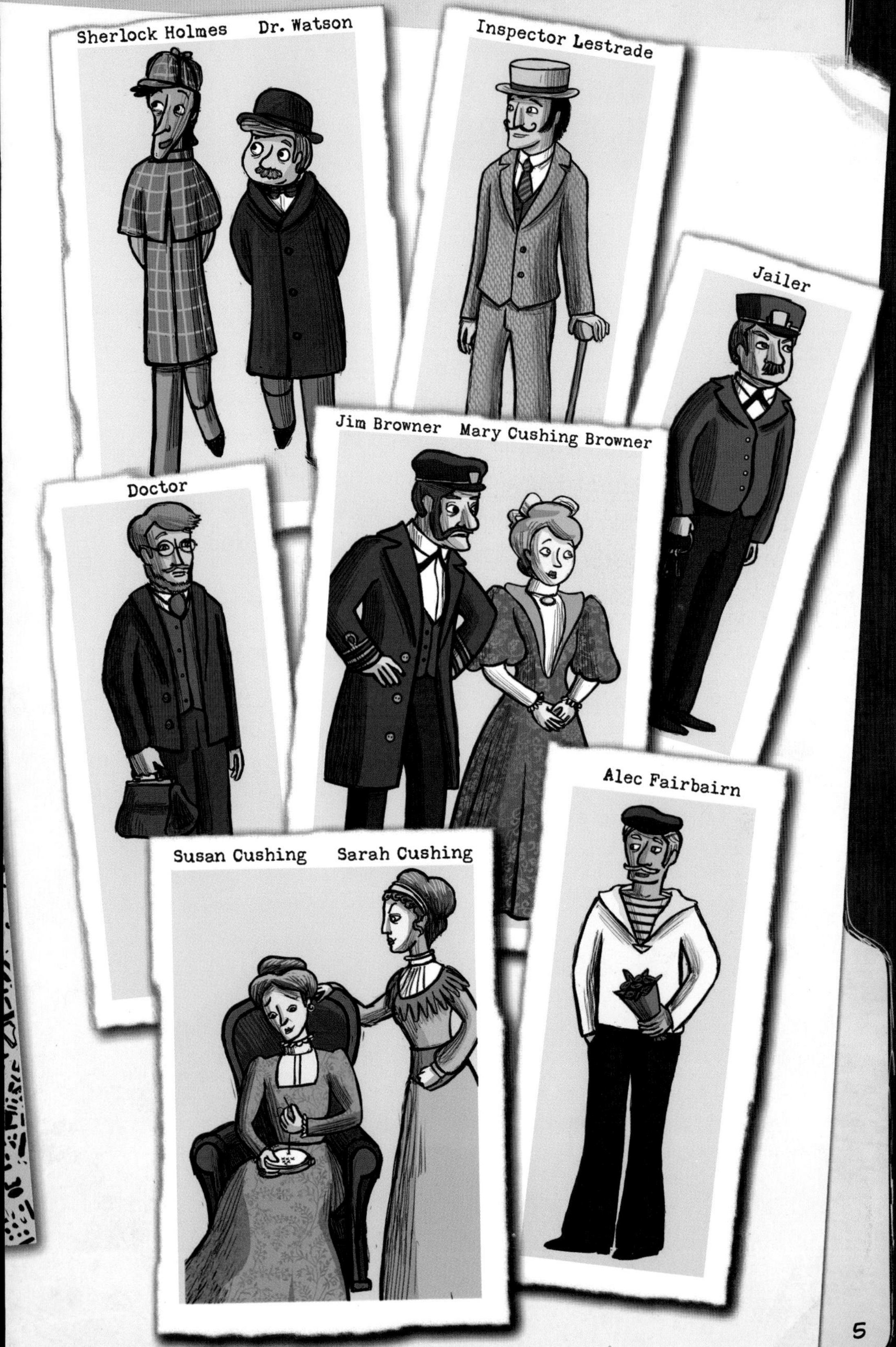
Sherlock Holmes
Dr. Watson
Inspector Lestrade
Jailer
Jim Browner
Mary Cushing Browner
Doctor
Alec Fairbairn
Susan Cushing
Sarah Cushing

From the Desk of John H. Watson, M.D.

My name is Dr. John H. Watson. For several years, I have been assisting my friend, Sherlock Holmes, in solving mysteries throughout the bustling city of London and beyond. Holmes is a peculiar man—always questioning and reasoning his way through various problems. But, when I first met him in 1878, I was immediately intrigued by his oddities.

Holmes has always been more daring than I and his logical deduction never ceases to amaze me. I have begun writing down all of the adventures I have with Holmes. This is one of those stories.

Sincerely,

Dr. Watson

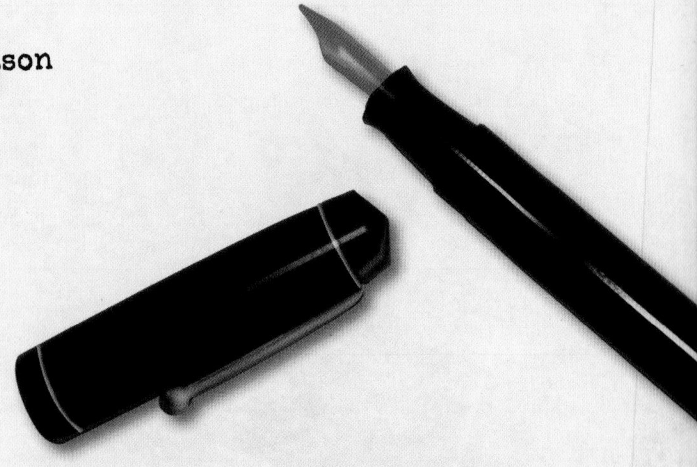

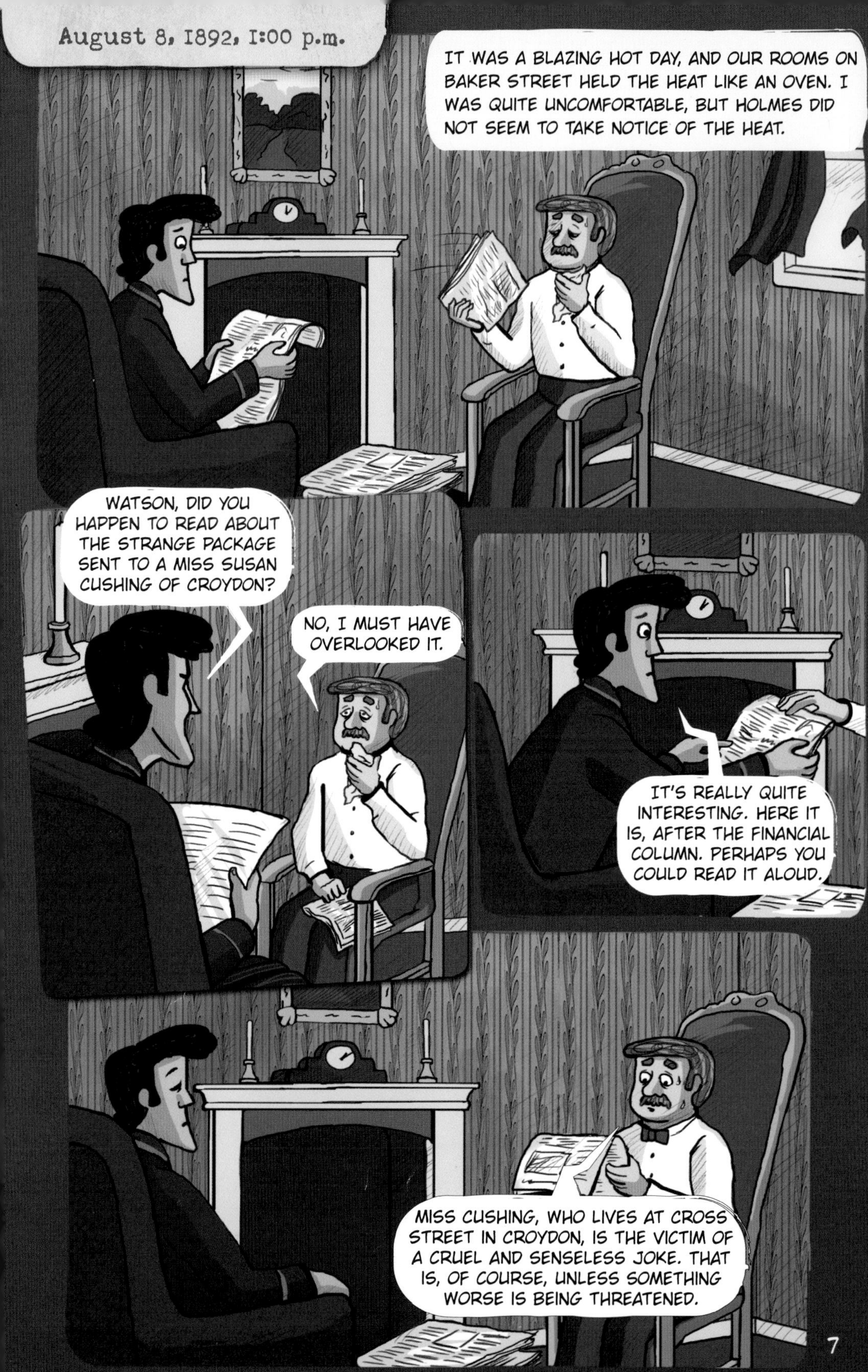
August 8, 1892, 1:00 p.m.
IT WAS A BLAZING HOT DAY, AND OUR ROOMS ON BAKER STREET HELD THE HEAT LIKE AN OVEN. I WAS QUITE UNCOMFORTABLE, BUT HOLMES DID NOT SEEM TO TAKE NOTICE OF THE HEAT.
WATSON, DID YOU HAPPEN TO READ ABOUT THE STRANGE PACKAGE SENT TO A MISS SUSAN CUSHING OF CROYDON?
NO, I MUST HAVE OVERLOOKED IT.
IT'S REALLY QUITE INTERESTING. HERE IT IS, AFTER THE FINANCIAL COLUMN. PERHAPS YOU COULD READ IT ALOUD.
MISS CUSHING, WHO LIVES AT CROSS STREET IN CROYDON, IS THE VICTIM OF A CRUEL AND SENSELESS JOKE. THAT IS, OF COURSE, UNLESS SOMETHING WORSE IS BEING THREATENED.

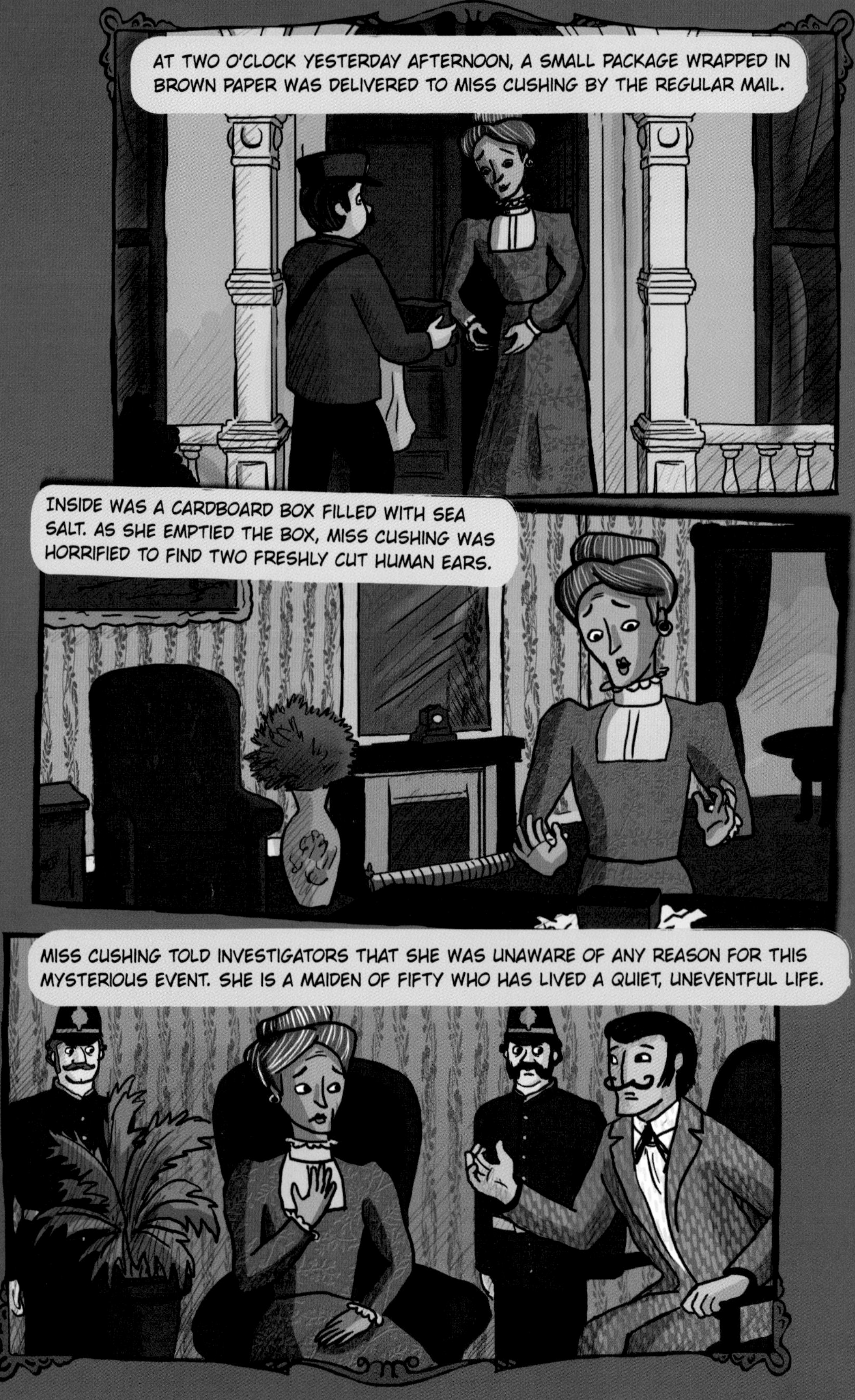
AT TWO O'CLOCK YESTERDAY AFTERNOON, A SMALL PACKAGE WRAPPED IN BROWN PAPER WAS DELIVERED TO MISS CUSHING BY THE REGULAR MAIL.
INSIDE WAS A CARDBOARD BOX FILLED WITH SEA SALT. AS SHE EMPTIED THE BOX, MISS CUSHING WAS HORRIFIED TO FIND TWO FRESHLY CUT HUMAN EARS.
MISS CUSHING TOLD INVESTIGATORS THAT SHE WAS UNAWARE OF ANY REASON FOR THIS MYSTERIOUS EVENT. SHE IS A MAIDEN OF FIFTY WHO HAS LIVED A QUIET, UNEVENTFUL LIFE.

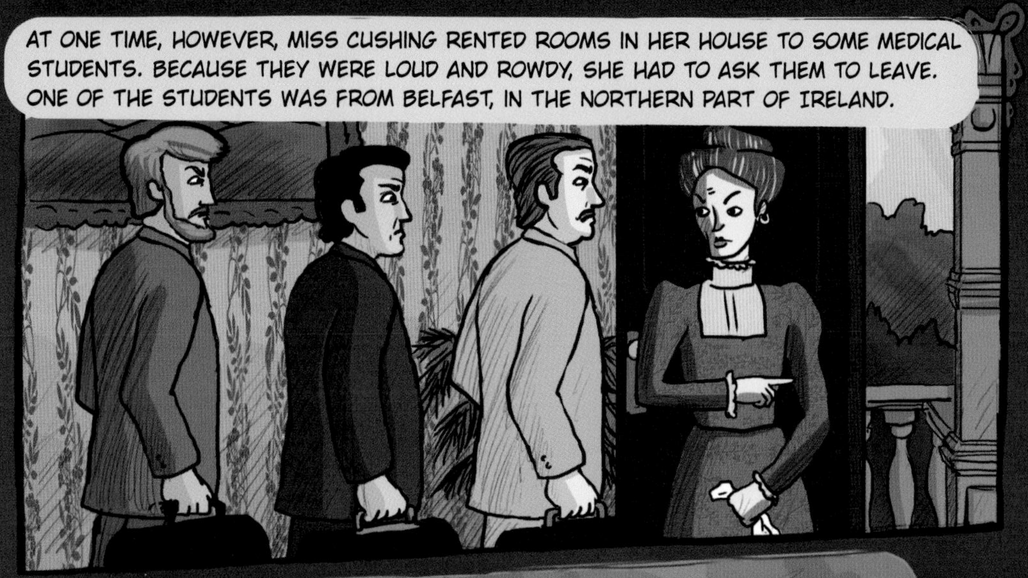
AT ONE TIME, HOWEVER, MISS CUSHING RENTED ROOMS IN HER HOUSE TO SOME MEDICAL STUDENTS. BECAUSE THEY WERE LOUD AND ROWDY, SHE HAD TO ASK THEM TO LEAVE. ONE OF THE STUDENTS WAS FROM BELFAST, IN THE NORTHERN PART OF IRELAND.

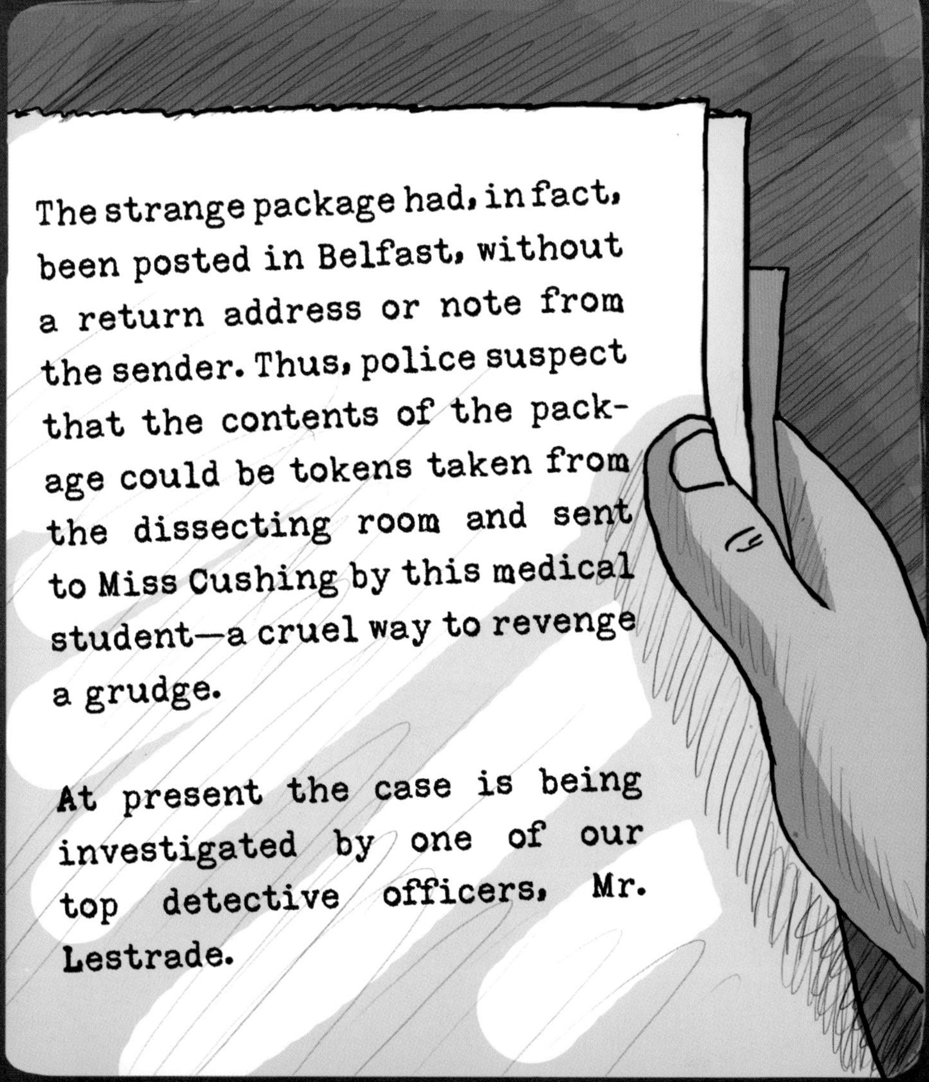
The strange package had, in fact, been posted in Belfast, without a return address or note from the sender. Thus, police suspect that the contents of the package could be tokens taken from the dissecting room and sent to Miss Cushing by this medical student—a cruel way to revenge a grudge.
At present the case is being investigated by one of our top detective officers, Mr. Lestrade.

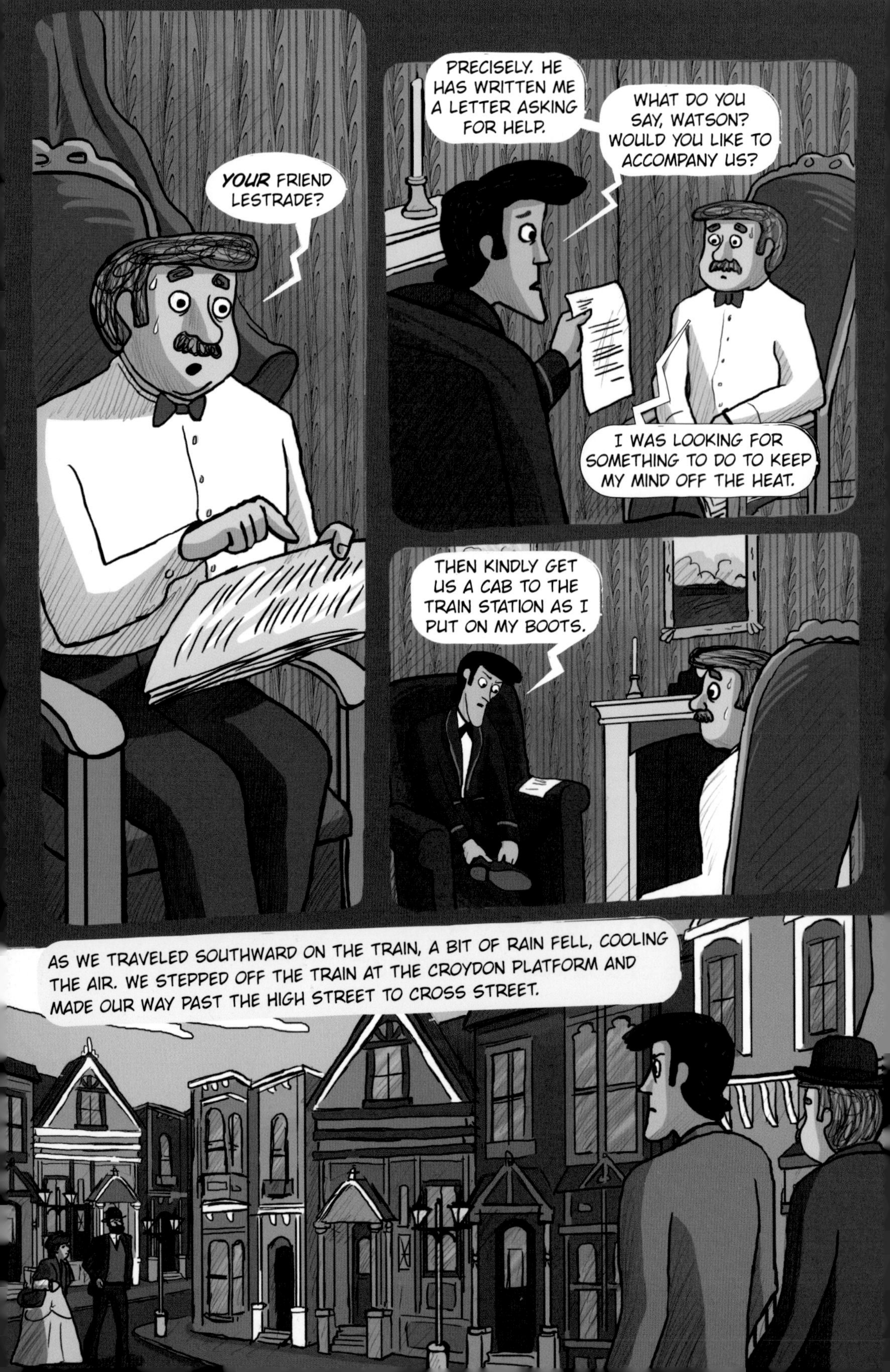
YOUR FRIEND LESTRADE?
PRECISELY. HE HAS WRITTEN ME A LETTER ASKING FOR HELP.
WHAT DO YOU SAY, WATSON? WOULD YOU LIKE TO ACCOMPANY US?
I WAS LOOKING FOR SOMETHING TO DO TO KEEP MY MIND OFF THE HEAT.
THEN KINDLY GET US A CAB TO THE TRAIN STATION AS I PUT ON MY BOOTS.
AS WE TRAVELED SOUTHWARD ON THE TRAIN, A BIT OF RAIN FELL, COOLING THE AIR. WE STEPPED OFF THE TRAIN AT THE CROYDON PLATFORM AND MADE OUR WAY PAST THE HIGH STREET TO CROSS STREET.

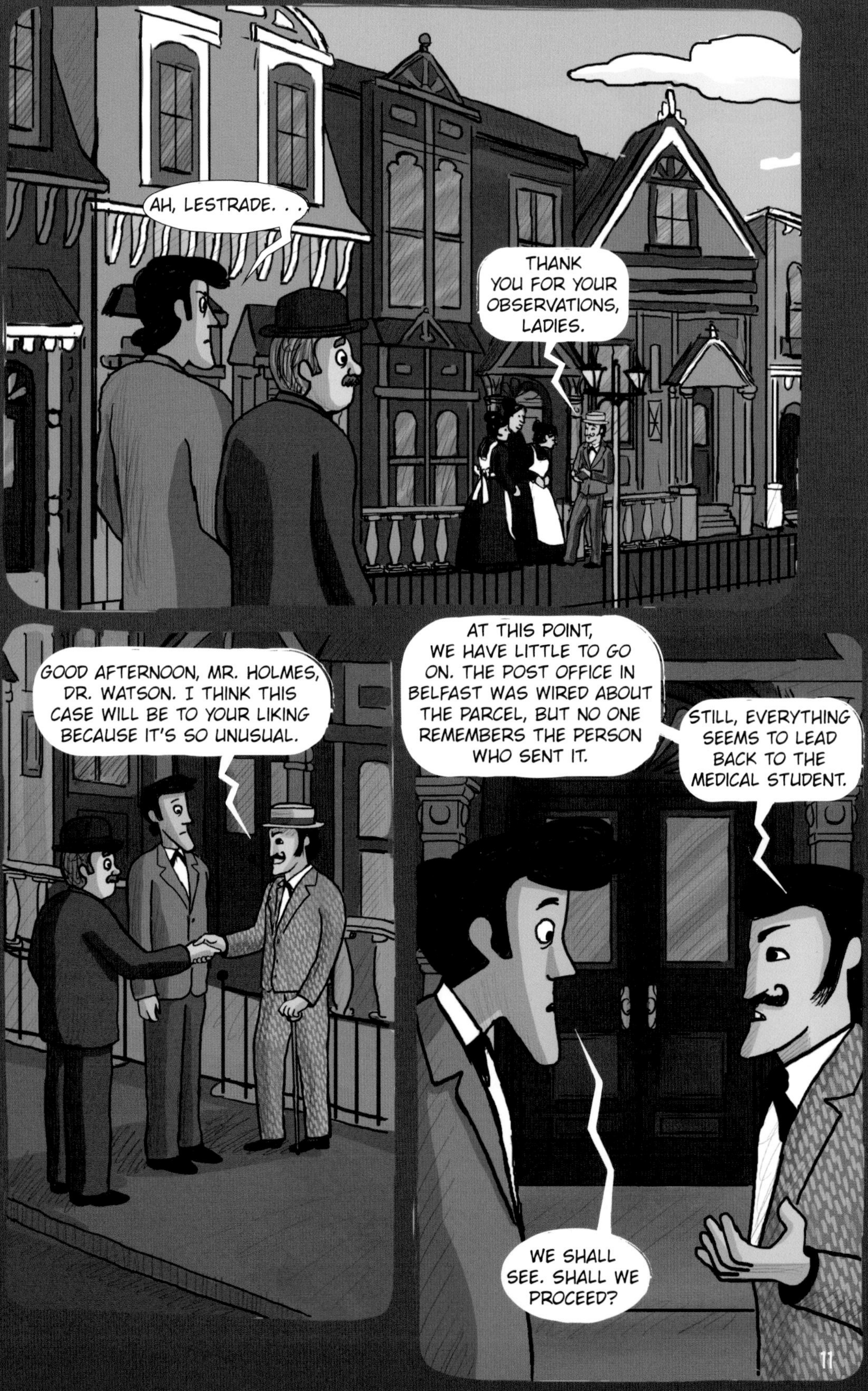
AH, LESTRADE. . .
THANK YOU FOR YOUR OBSERVATIONS, LADIES.
GOOD AFTERNOON, MR. HOLMES, DR. WATSON. I THINK THIS CASE WILL BE TO YOUR LIKING BECAUSE IT'S SO UNUSUAL.
AT THIS POINT, WE HAVE LITTLE TO GO ON. THE POST OFFICE IN BELFAST WAS WIRED ABOUT THE PARCEL, BUT NO ONE REMEMBERS THE PERSON WHO SENT IT.
STILL, EVERYTHING SEEMS TO LEAD BACK TO THE MEDICAL STUDENT.
WE SHALL SEE. SHALL WE PROCEED?

Lestrade tapped at the door. A young servant girl answered and brought us into a small front room. We felt the full force of the summer heat in the room. In a chair by the open window, Miss Cushing sat embroidering.

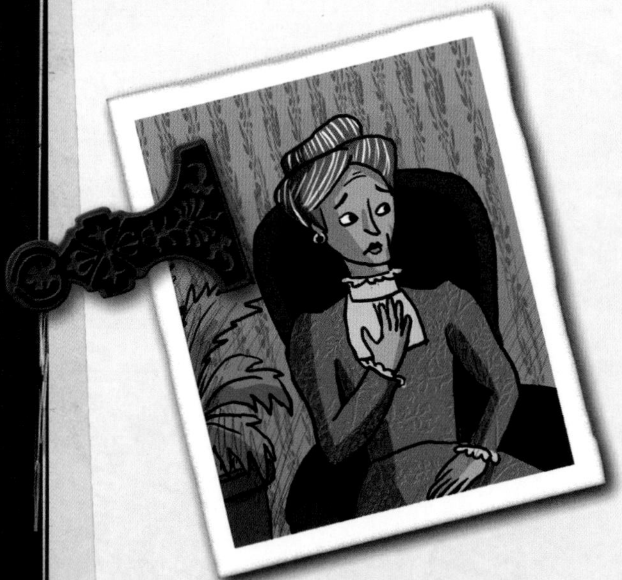

YOU'LL FIND THOSE **DREADFUL THINGS** IN THE SHED OUT BACK, INSPECTOR, NOT IN MY HOME.
MISS CUSHING, I HAVE ONLY RETURNED SO THAT MY FRIEND MR. HOLMES COULD TAKE A LOOK AT THE PARCEL AND ASK YOU A FEW QUESTIONS.
WHY DO YOU NEED TO ASK ME MORE QUESTIONS? I'VE TOLD YOU I KNOW NOTHING.
AND I AM NOT ACCUSTOMED TO ALL THIS COMMOTION. I DISLIKE HAVING MY NAME IN THE PAPERS AND THE POLICE IN MY HOUSE.
MISS CUSHING, WE WILL DISTURB YOU AS LITTLE AS POSSIBLE.
GO PLEASE LOOK FOR YOURSELF THEN. I JUST WANT TO GET PAST THIS AWFUL MESS.

L estrade went into the small garden shed. He came out carrying a yellow cardboard box, a piece of brown wrapping paper, and some string. We sat on the garden bench. Holmes began examining the articles.

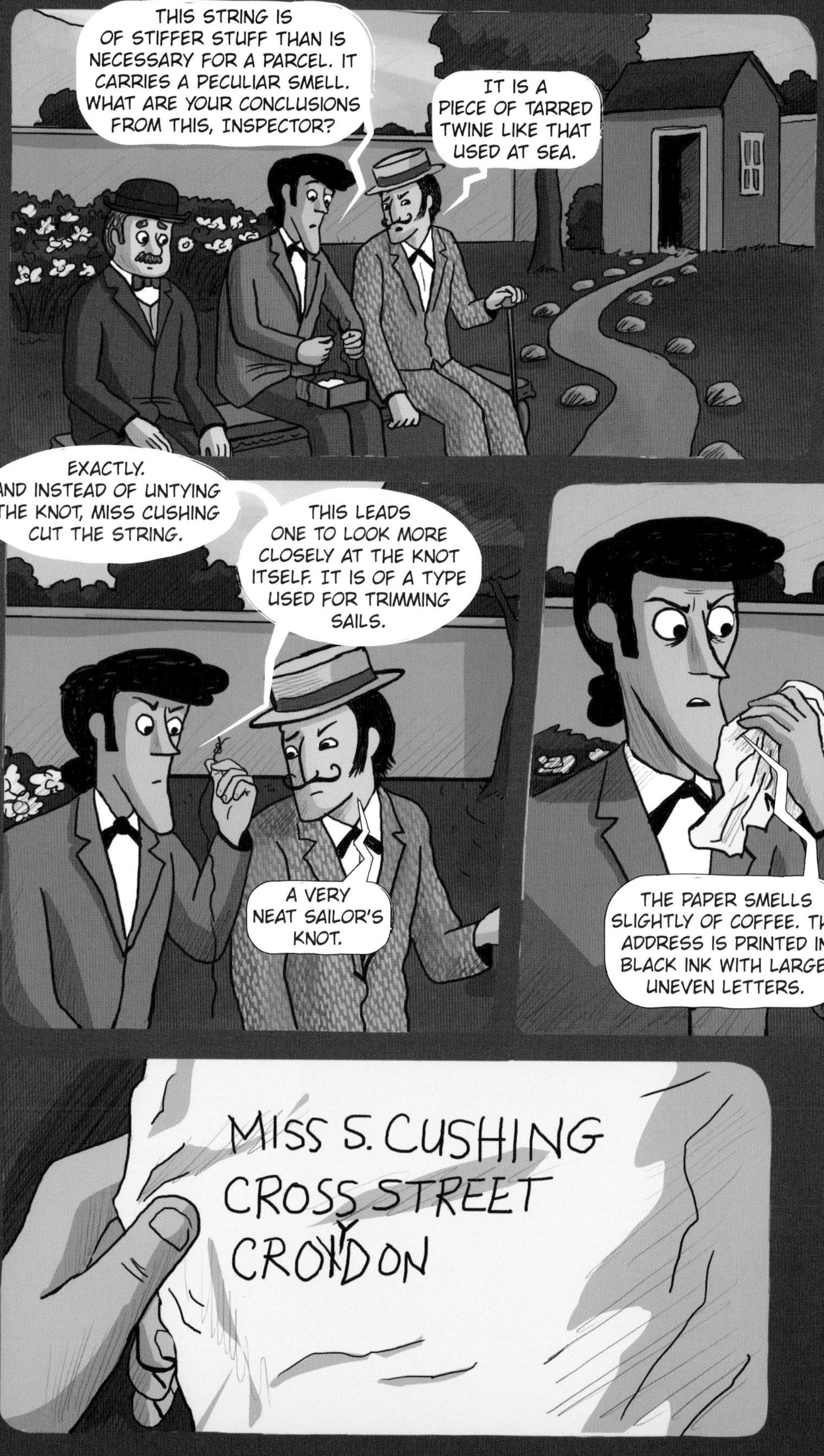
THIS STRING IS OF STIFFER STUFF THAN IS NECESSARY FOR A PARCEL. IT CARRIES A PECULIAR SMELL. WHAT ARE YOUR CONCLUSIONS FROM THIS, INSPECTOR?
IT IS A PIECE OF TARRED TWINE LIKE THAT USED AT SEA.
EXACTLY. AND INSTEAD OF UNTYING THE KNOT, MISS CUSHING CUT THE STRING.
THIS LEADS ONE TO LOOK MORE CLOSELY AT THE KNOT ITSELF. IT IS OF A TYPE USED FOR TRIMMING SAILS.
A VERY NEAT SAILOR'S KNOT.
THE PAPER SMELLS SLIGHTLY OF COFFEE. THE ADDRESS IS PRINTED IN BLACK INK WITH LARGE, UNEVEN LETTERS.
MISS S. CUSHING
CROSS STREET
CROYDON

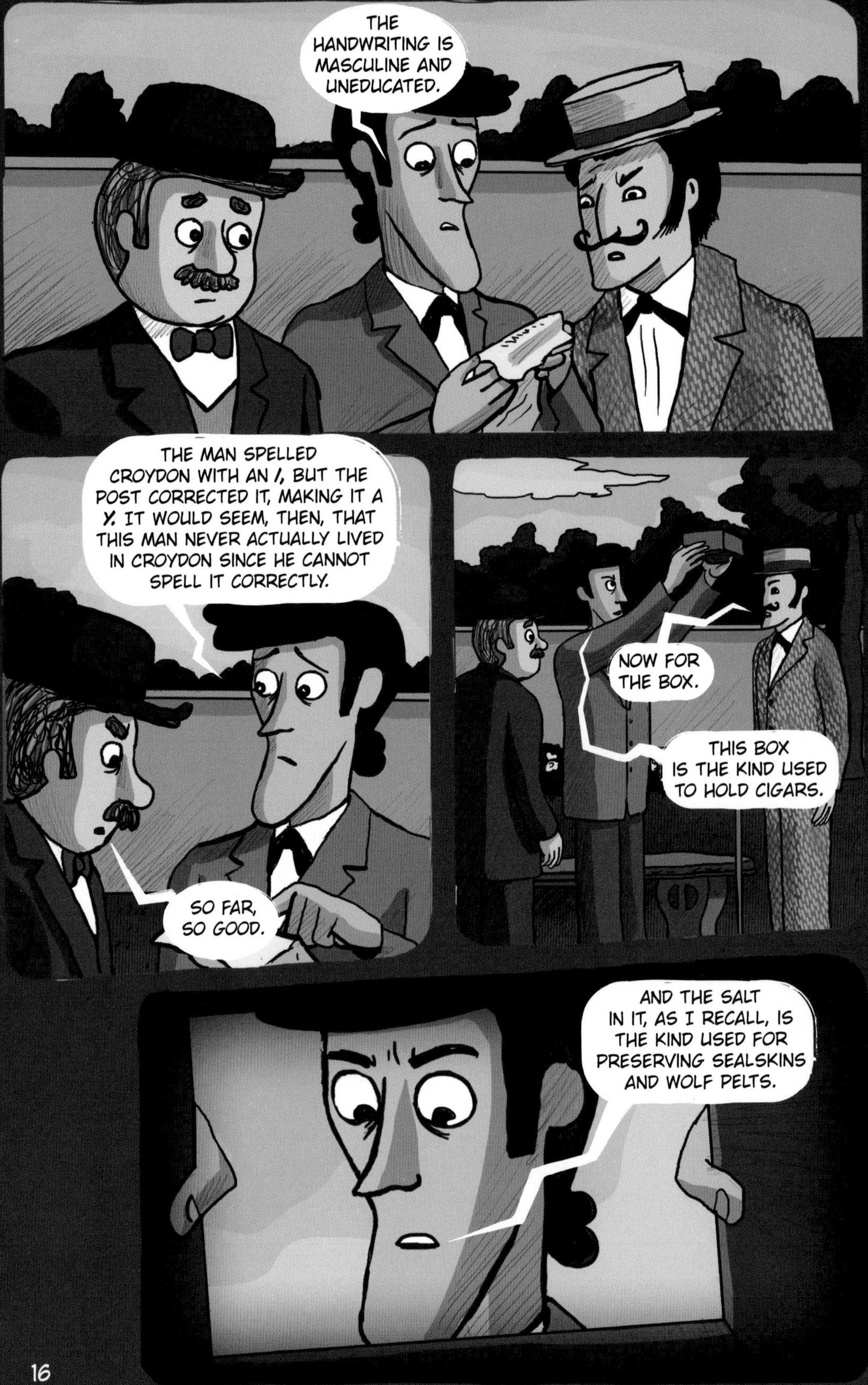
THE HANDWRITING IS MASCULINE AND UNEDUCATED.
THE MAN SPELLED CROYDON WITH AN I, BUT THE POST CORRECTED IT, MAKING IT A Y. IT WOULD SEEM, THEN, THAT THIS MAN NEVER ACTUALLY LIVED IN CROYDON SINCE HE CANNOT SPELL IT CORRECTLY.
SO FAR, SO GOOD.
NOW FOR THE BOX.
THIS BOX IS THE KIND USED TO HOLD CIGARS.
AND THE SALT IN IT, AS I RECALL, IS THE KIND USED FOR PRESERVING SEALSKINS AND WOLF PELTS.

On top of the large salt crystals were two ears of different sizes. One was small and fine, with a slight pink color. The other was larger and sunburned. Both were pierced for earrings.

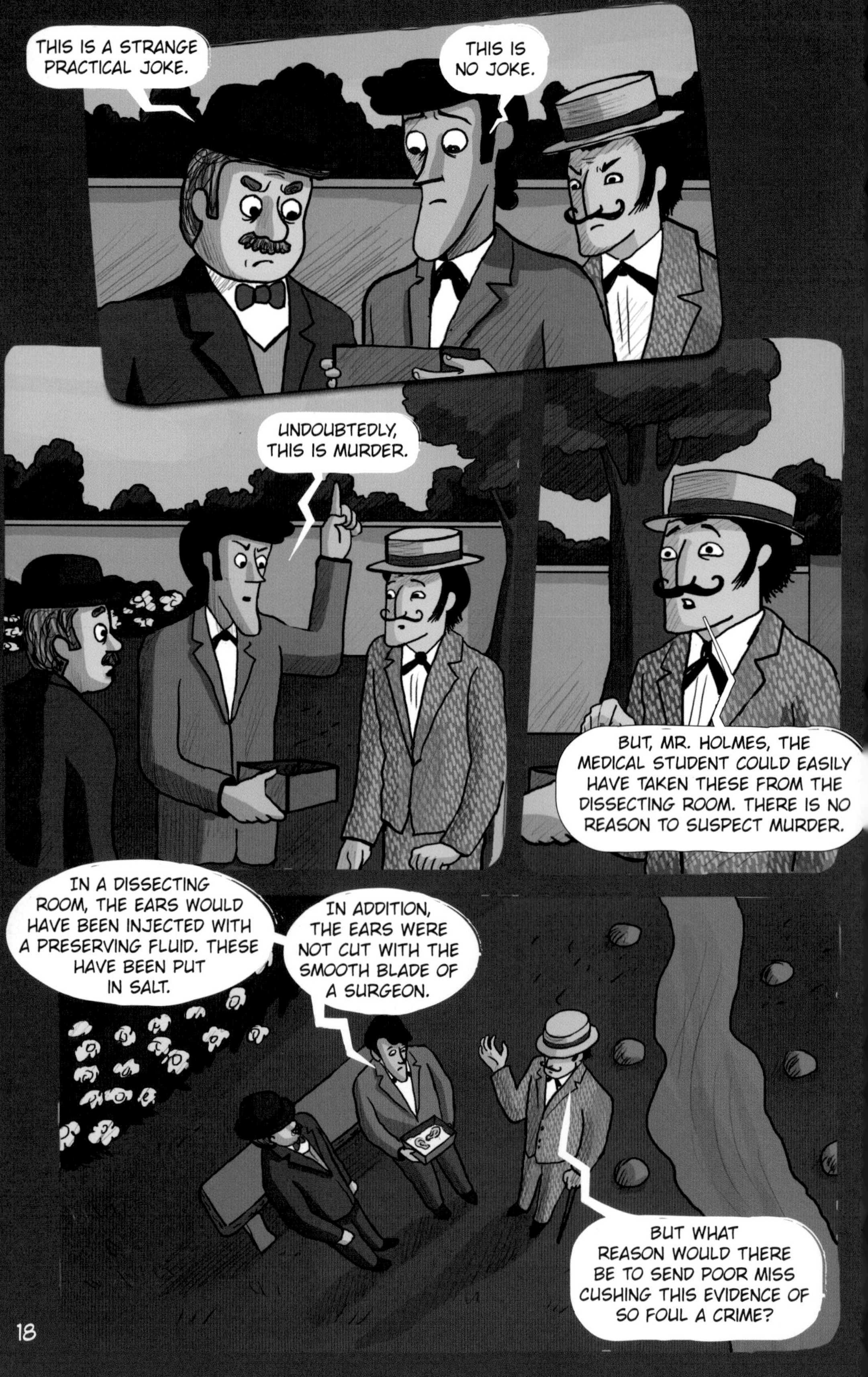

THIS IS A STRANGE PRACTICAL JOKE.
THIS IS NO JOKE.
UNDOUBTEDLY, THIS IS MURDER.
BUT, MR. HOLMES, THE MEDICAL STUDENT COULD EASILY HAVE TAKEN THESE FROM THE DISSECTING ROOM. THERE IS NO REASON TO SUSPECT MURDER.
IN A DISSECTING ROOM, THE EARS WOULD HAVE BEEN INJECTED WITH A PRESERVING FLUID. THESE HAVE BEEN PUT IN SALT.
IN ADDITION, THE EARS WERE NOT CUT WITH THE SMOOTH BLADE OF A SURGEON.
BUT WHAT REASON WOULD THERE BE TO SEND POOR MISS CUSHING THIS EVIDENCE OF SO FOUL A CRIME?

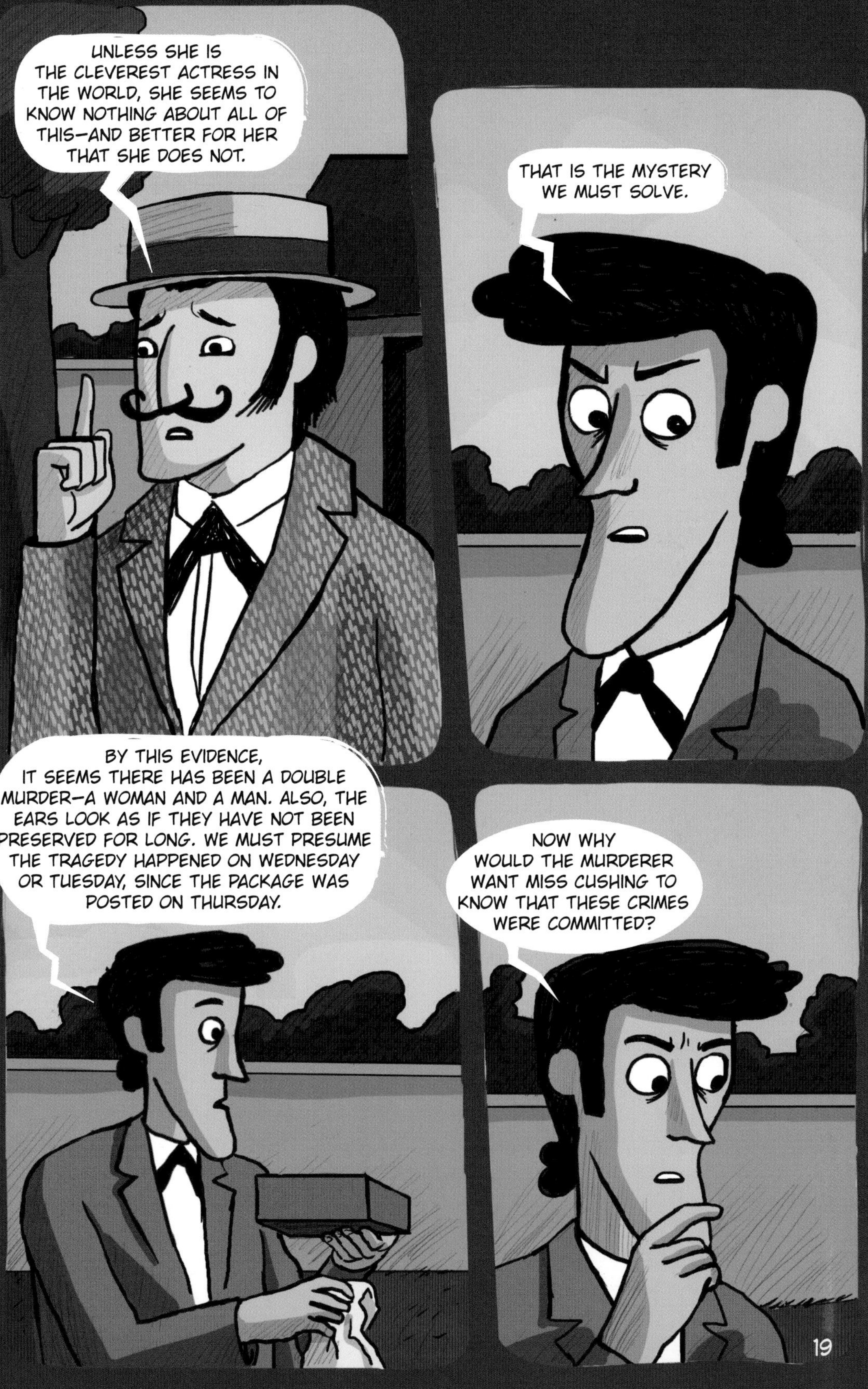
UNLESS SHE IS THE CLEVEREST ACTRESS IN THE WORLD, SHE SEEMS TO KNOW NOTHING ABOUT ALL OF THIS—AND BETTER FOR HER THAT SHE DOES NOT.
THAT IS THE MYSTERY WE MUST SOLVE.
BY THIS EVIDENCE, IT SEEMS THERE HAS BEEN A DOUBLE MURDER—A WOMAN AND A MAN. ALSO, THE EARS LOOK AS IF THEY HAVE NOT BEEN PRESERVED FOR LONG. WE MUST PRESUME THE TRAGEDY HAPPENED ON WEDNESDAY OR TUESDAY, SINCE THE PACKAGE WAS POSTED ON THURSDAY.
NOW WHY WOULD THE MURDERER WANT MISS CUSHING TO KNOW THAT THESE CRIMES WERE COMMITTED?

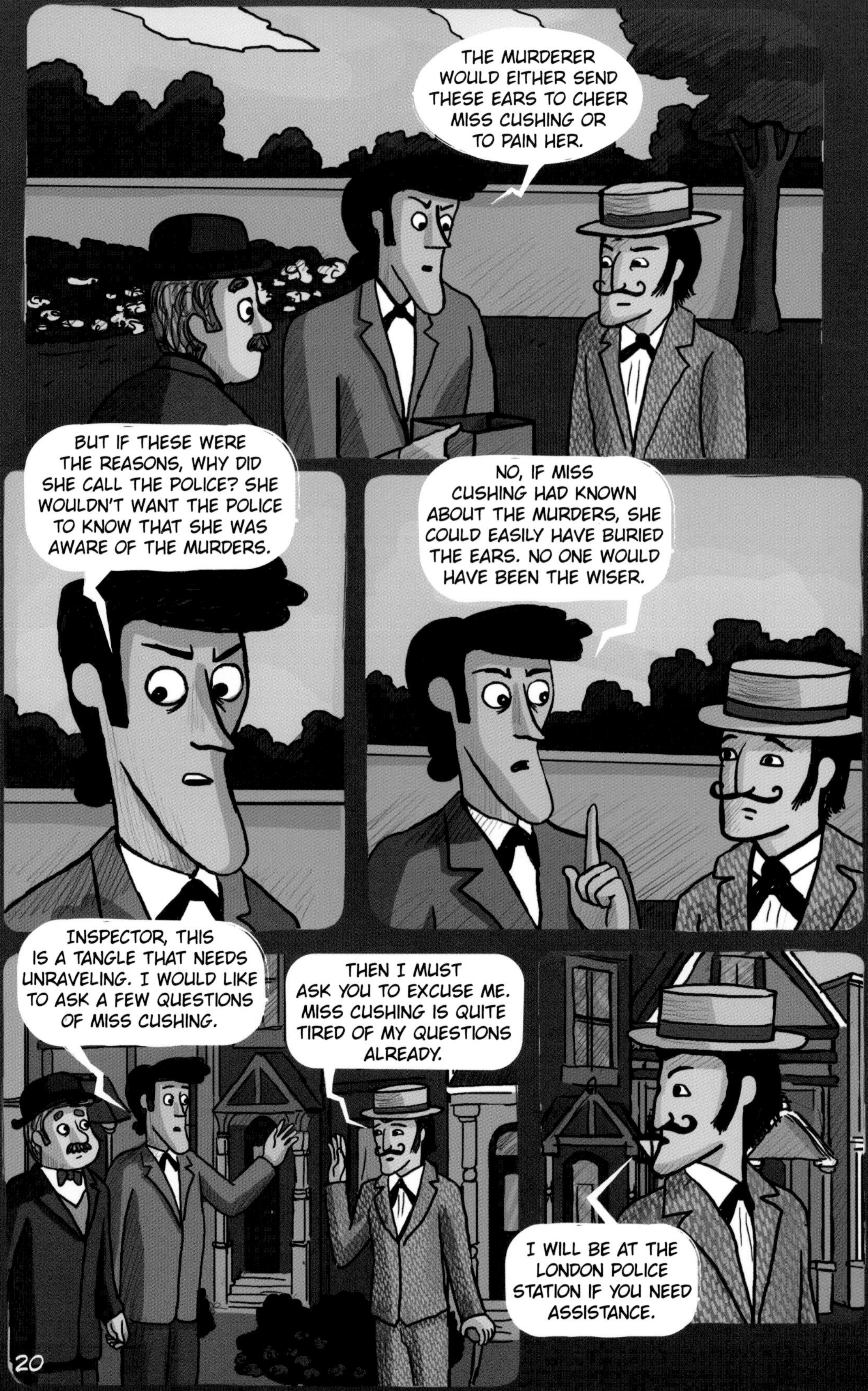
THE MURDERER WOULD EITHER SEND THESE EARS TO CHEER MISS CUSHING OR TO PAIN HER.
BUT IF THESE WERE THE REASONS, WHY DID SHE CALL THE POLICE? SHE WOULDN'T WANT THE POLICE TO KNOW THAT SHE WAS AWARE OF THE MURDERS.
NO, IF MISS CUSHING HAD KNOWN ABOUT THE MURDERS, SHE COULD EASILY HAVE BURIED THE EARS. NO ONE WOULD HAVE BEEN THE WISER.
INSPECTOR, THIS IS A TANGLE THAT NEEDS UNRAVELING. I WOULD LIKE TO ASK A FEW QUESTIONS OF MISS CUSHING.
THEN I MUST ASK YOU TO EXCUSE ME. MISS CUSHING IS QUITE TIRED OF MY QUESTIONS ALREADY.
I WILL BE AT THE LONDON POLICE STATION IF YOU NEED ASSISTANCE.

After Inspector Lestrade departed, we headed for the back door. As we walked into the front room, we saw Miss Cushing staring absently out the window. The afternoon sun shone down on her, glinting off her fine loop earrings and the emerald ring on her right hand. Holmes paused in his step and stared at her profile. She turned when she sensed our presence.

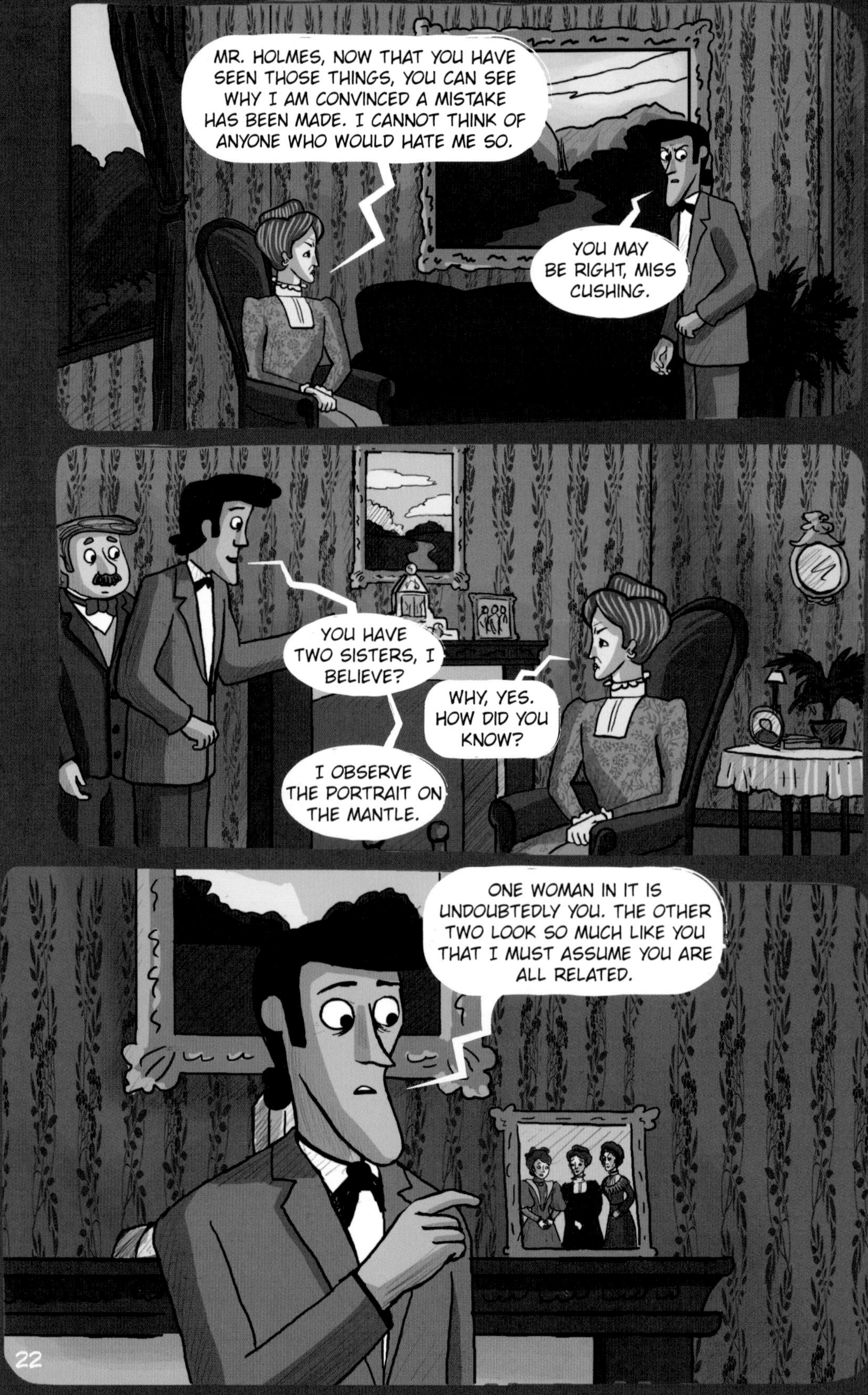
MR. HOLMES, NOW THAT YOU HAVE SEEN THOSE THINGS, YOU CAN SEE WHY I AM CONVINCED A MISTAKE HAS BEEN MADE. I CANNOT THINK OF ANYONE WHO WOULD HATE ME SO.
YOU MAY BE RIGHT, MISS CUSHING.
YOU HAVE TWO SISTERS, I BELIEVE?
WHY, YES. HOW DID YOU KNOW?
I OBSERVE THE PORTRAIT ON THE MANTLE.
ONE WOMAN IN IT IS UNDOUBTEDLY YOU. THE OTHER TWO LOOK SO MUCH LIKE YOU THAT I MUST ASSUME YOU ARE ALL RELATED.

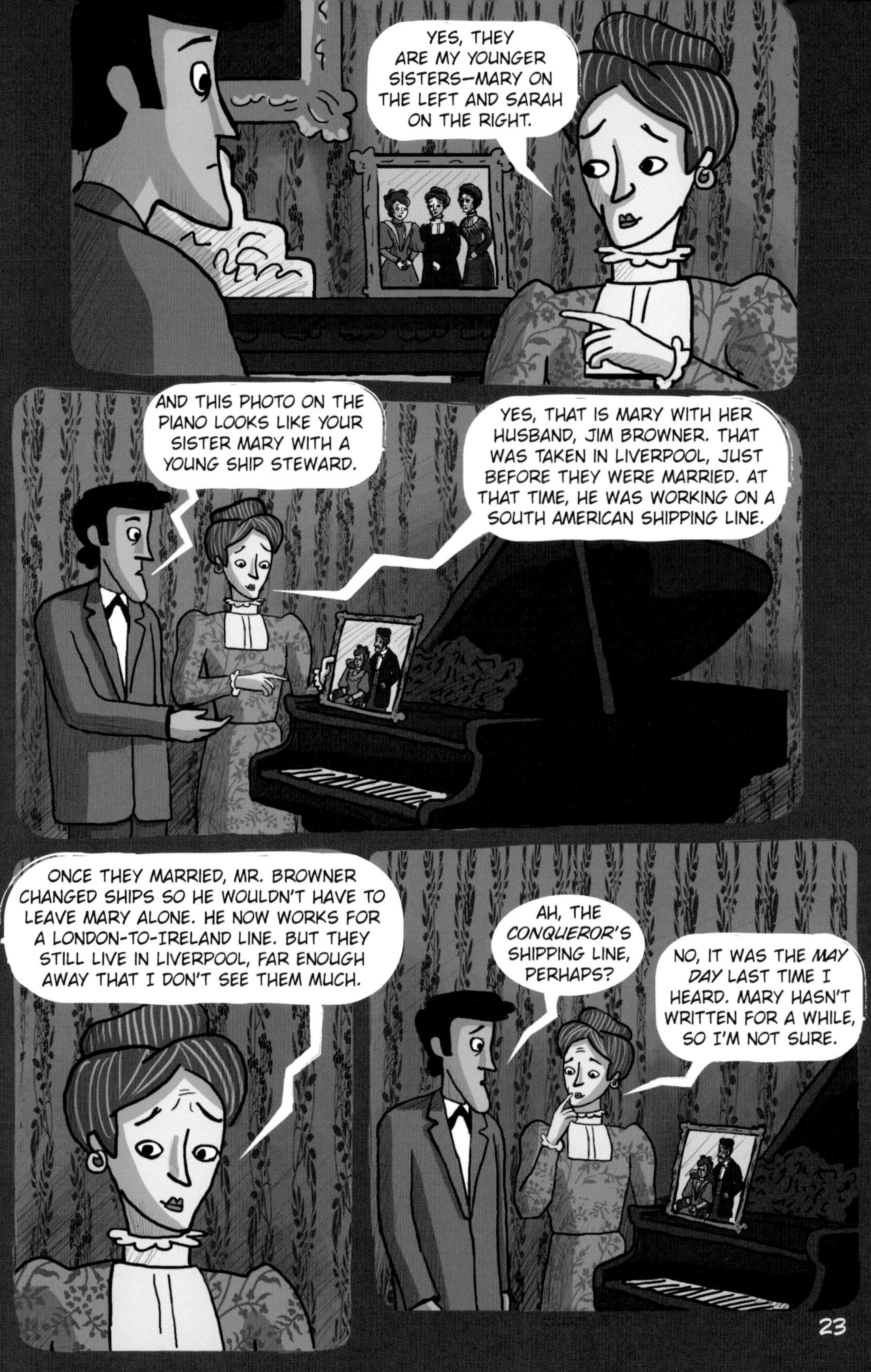
YES, THEY ARE MY YOUNGER SISTERS—MARY ON THE LEFT AND SARAH ON THE RIGHT.
AND THIS PHOTO ON THE PIANO LOOKS LIKE YOUR SISTER MARY WITH A YOUNG SHIP STEWARD.
YES, THAT IS MARY WITH HER HUSBAND, JIM BROWNER. THAT WAS TAKEN IN LIVERPOOL, JUST BEFORE THEY WERE MARRIED. AT THAT TIME, HE WAS WORKING ON A SOUTH AMERICAN SHIPPING LINE.
ONCE THEY MARRIED, MR. BROWNER CHANGED SHIPS SO HE WOULDN'T HAVE TO LEAVE MARY ALONE. HE NOW WORKS FOR A LONDON-TO-IRELAND LINE. BUT THEY STILL LIVE IN LIVERPOOL, FAR ENOUGH AWAY THAT I DON'T SEE THEM MUCH.
AH, THE *CONQUEROR*'S SHIPPING LINE, PERHAPS?
NO, IT WAS THE *MAY DAY* LAST TIME I HEARD. MARY HASN'T WRITTEN FOR A WHILE, SO I'M NOT SURE.

Miss Cushing talked easily now, like a lonely person who has finally found an audience. She talked on about her sisters, her home, and the medical students who had caused her such trouble.

Holmes listened intently, asking a question here and there.

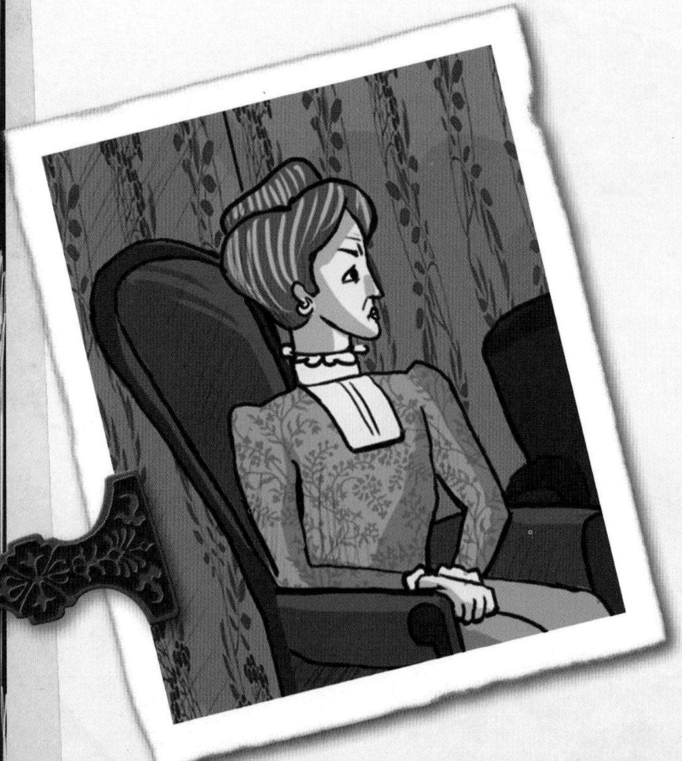

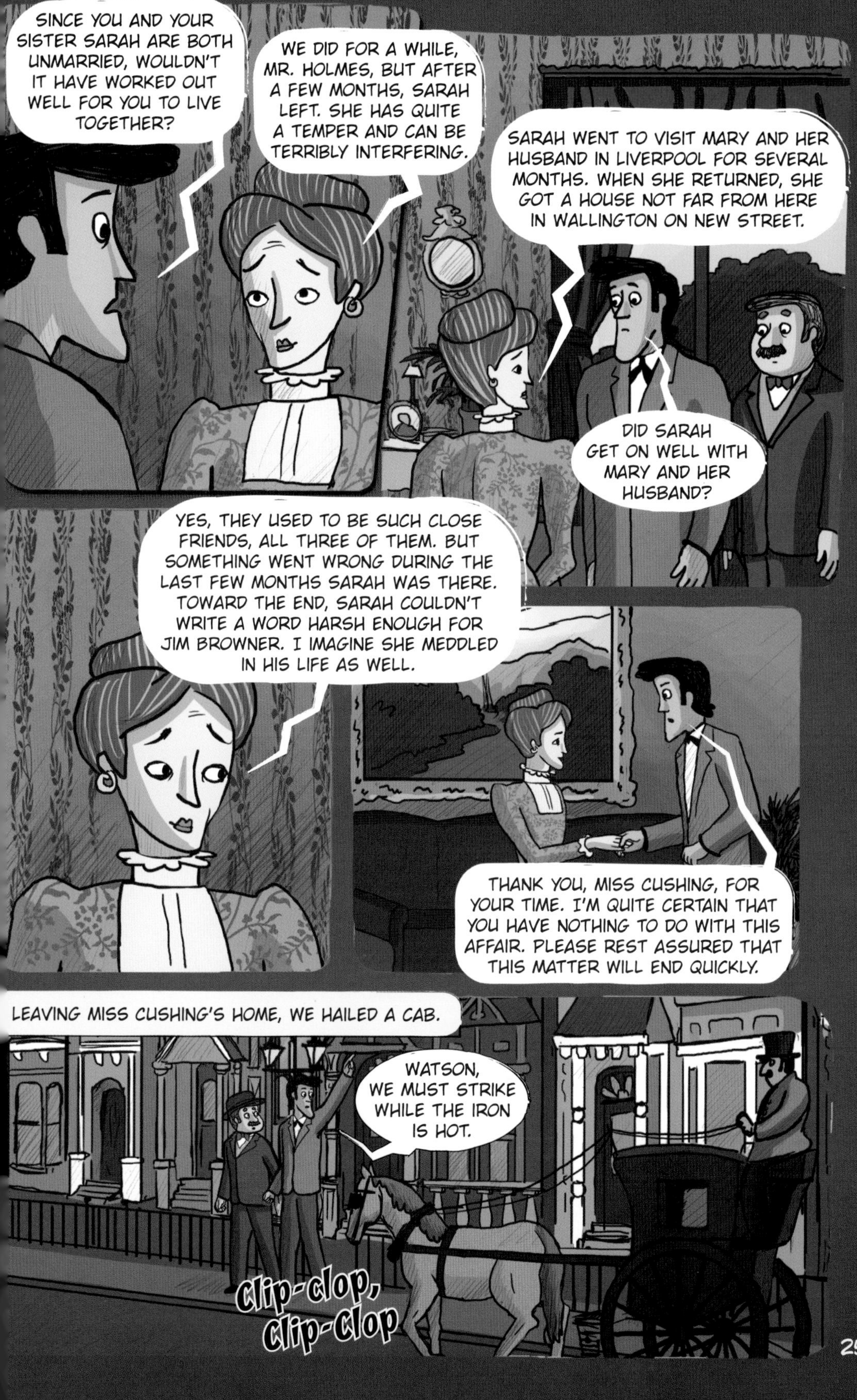
SINCE YOU AND YOUR SISTER SARAH ARE BOTH UNMARRIED, WOULDN'T IT HAVE WORKED OUT WELL FOR YOU TO LIVE TOGETHER?
WE DID FOR A WHILE, MR. HOLMES, BUT AFTER A FEW MONTHS, SARAH LEFT. SHE HAS QUITE A TEMPER AND CAN BE TERRIBLY INTERFERING.
SARAH WENT TO VISIT MARY AND HER HUSBAND IN LIVERPOOL FOR SEVERAL MONTHS. WHEN SHE RETURNED, SHE GOT A HOUSE NOT FAR FROM HERE IN WALLINGTON ON NEW STREET.
DID SARAH GET ON WELL WITH MARY AND HER HUSBAND?
YES, THEY USED TO BE SUCH CLOSE FRIENDS, ALL THREE OF THEM. BUT SOMETHING WENT WRONG DURING THE LAST FEW MONTHS SARAH WAS THERE. TOWARD THE END, SARAH COULDN'T WRITE A WORD HARSH ENOUGH FOR JIM BROWNER. I IMAGINE SHE MEDDLED IN HIS LIFE AS WELL.
THANK YOU, MISS CUSHING, FOR YOUR TIME. I'M QUITE CERTAIN THAT YOU HAVE NOTHING TO DO WITH THIS AFFAIR. PLEASE REST ASSURED THAT THIS MATTER WILL END QUICKLY.
LEAVING MISS CUSHING'S HOME, WE HAILED A CAB.
WATSON, WE MUST STRIKE WHILE THE IRON IS HOT.
Clip-clop, Clip-Clop

I was unsure what Holmes was talking about, but I followed his striding figure into the cab. We headed straight for the house of the other Miss Cushing. What, I thought, could Miss Sarah Cushing tell us about her sister's mysterious package?

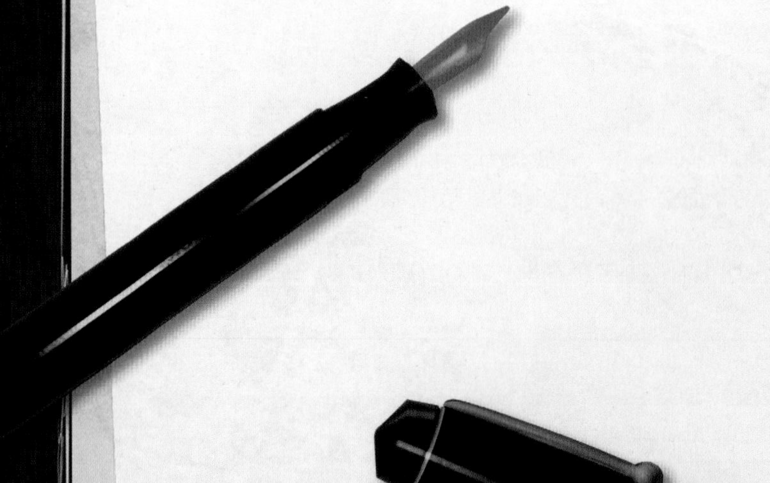

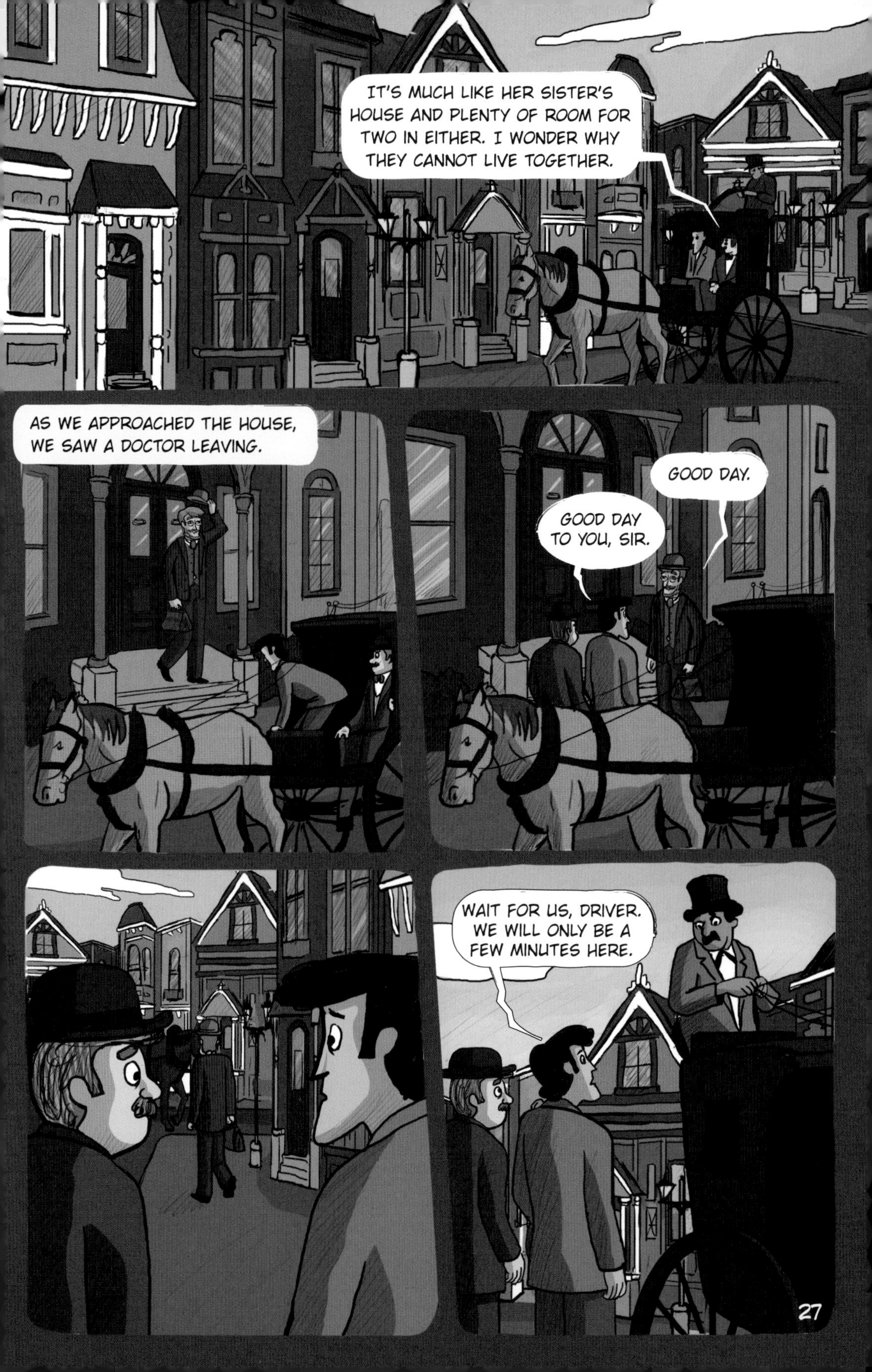
IT'S MUCH LIKE HER SISTER'S HOUSE AND PLENTY OF ROOM FOR TWO IN EITHER. I WONDER WHY THEY CANNOT LIVE TOGETHER.
AS WE APPROACHED THE HOUSE, WE SAW A DOCTOR LEAVING.
GOOD DAY.
GOOD DAY TO YOU, SIR.
WAIT FOR US, DRIVER. WE WILL ONLY BE A FEW MINUTES HERE.

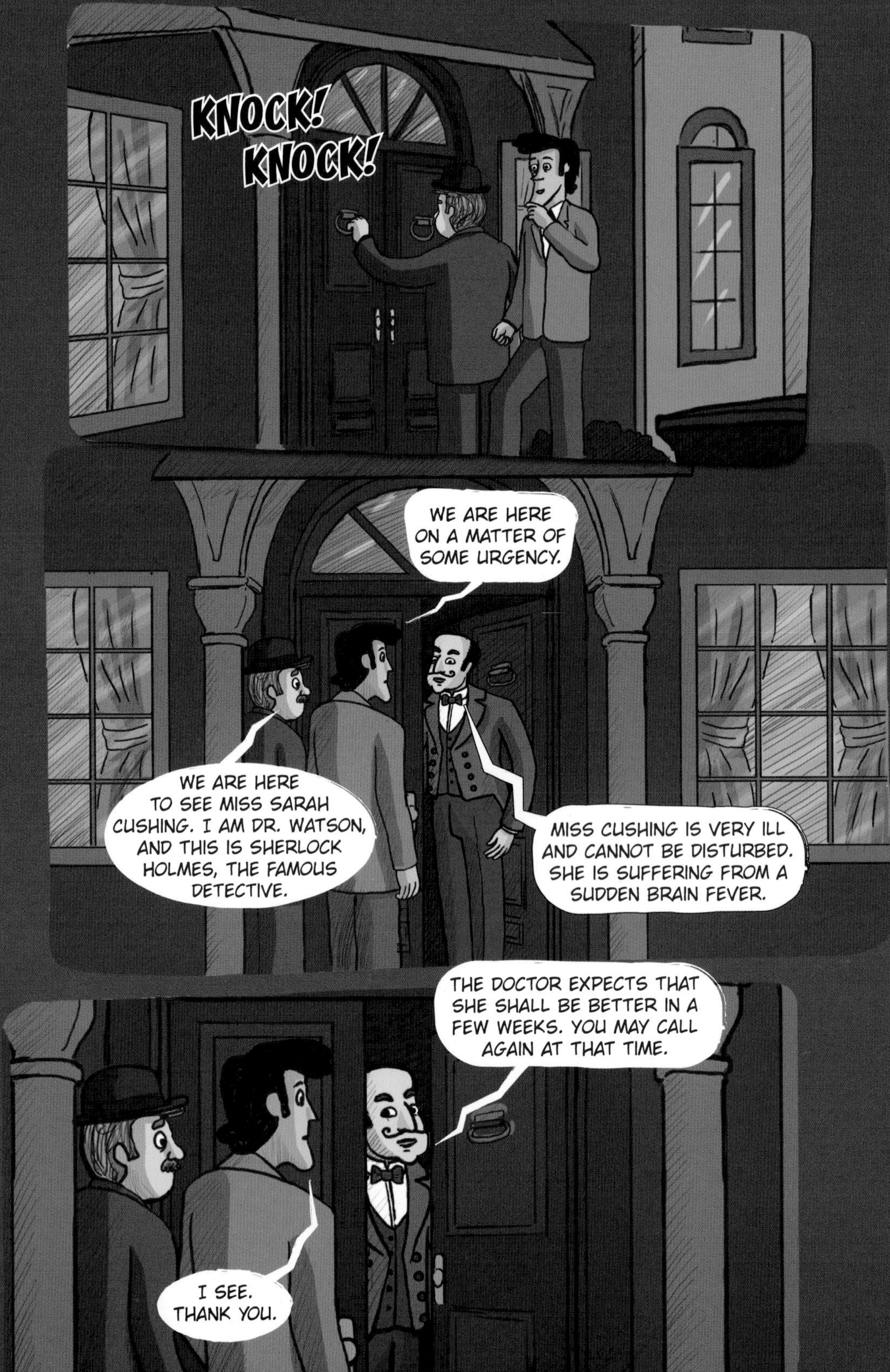
KNOCK! KNOCK!
WE ARE HERE ON A MATTER OF SOME URGENCY.
WE ARE HERE TO SEE MISS SARAH CUSHING. I AM DR. WATSON, AND THIS IS SHERLOCK HOLMES, THE FAMOUS DETECTIVE.
MISS CUSHING IS VERY ILL AND CANNOT BE DISTURBED. SHE IS SUFFERING FROM A SUDDEN BRAIN FEVER.
THE DOCTOR EXPECTS THAT SHE SHALL BE BETTER IN A FEW WEEKS. YOU MAY CALL AGAIN AT THAT TIME.
I SEE. THANK YOU.

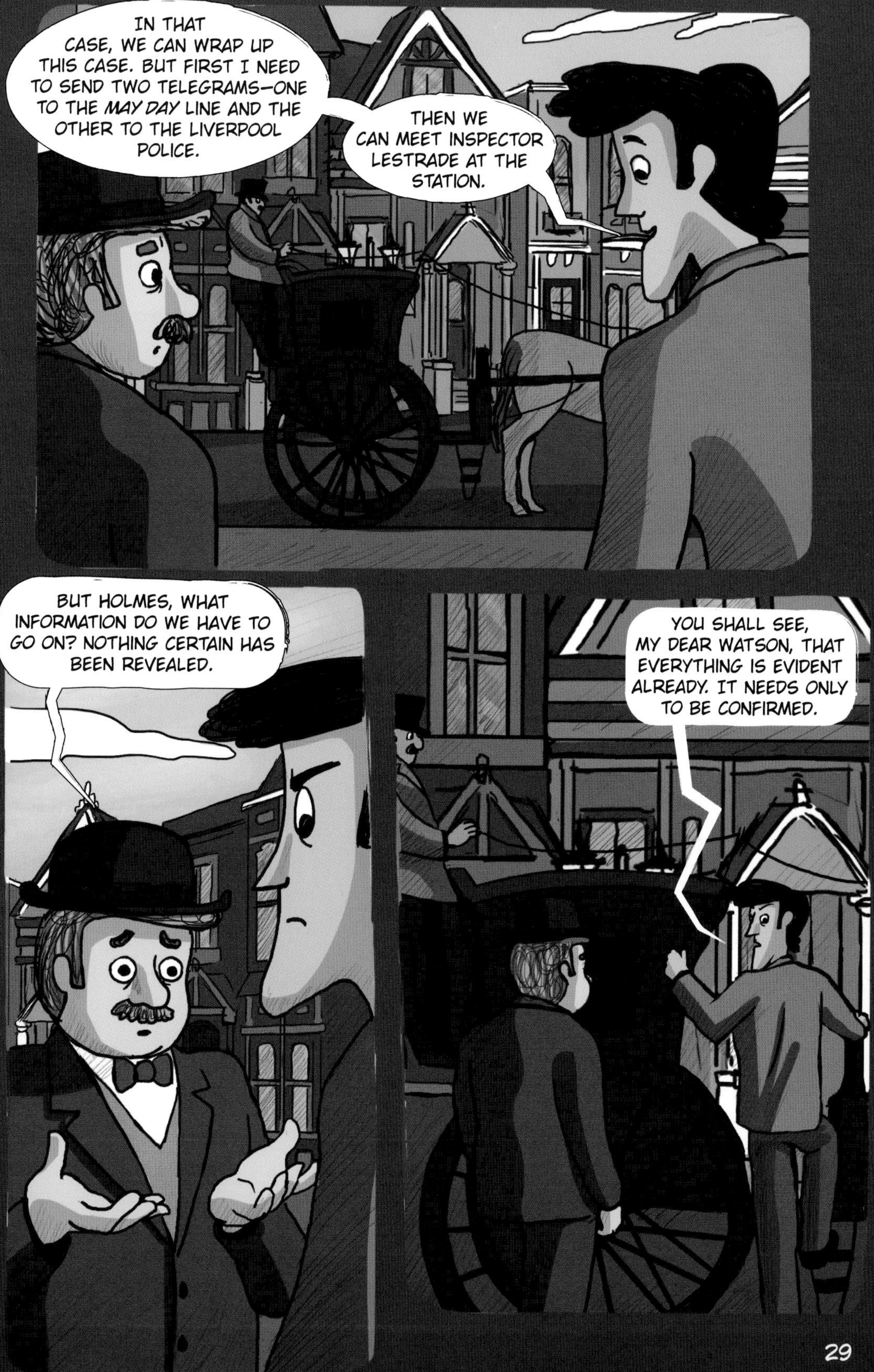
IN THAT CASE, WE CAN WRAP UP THIS CASE. BUT FIRST I NEED TO SEND TWO TELEGRAMS—ONE TO THE *MAY DAY* LINE AND THE OTHER TO THE LIVERPOOL POLICE.
THEN WE CAN MEET INSPECTOR LESTRADE AT THE STATION.
BUT HOLMES, WHAT INFORMATION DO WE HAVE TO GO ON? NOTHING CERTAIN HAS BEEN REVEALED.
YOU SHALL SEE, MY DEAR WATSON, THAT EVERYTHING IS EVIDENT ALREADY. IT NEEDS ONLY TO BE CONFIRMED.

As we headed to the train station, we stopped at a post office to send the telegrams and at a pub for a quick meal. By the time we arrived at the London police station, the sky had already taken on the warm glow of dusk.

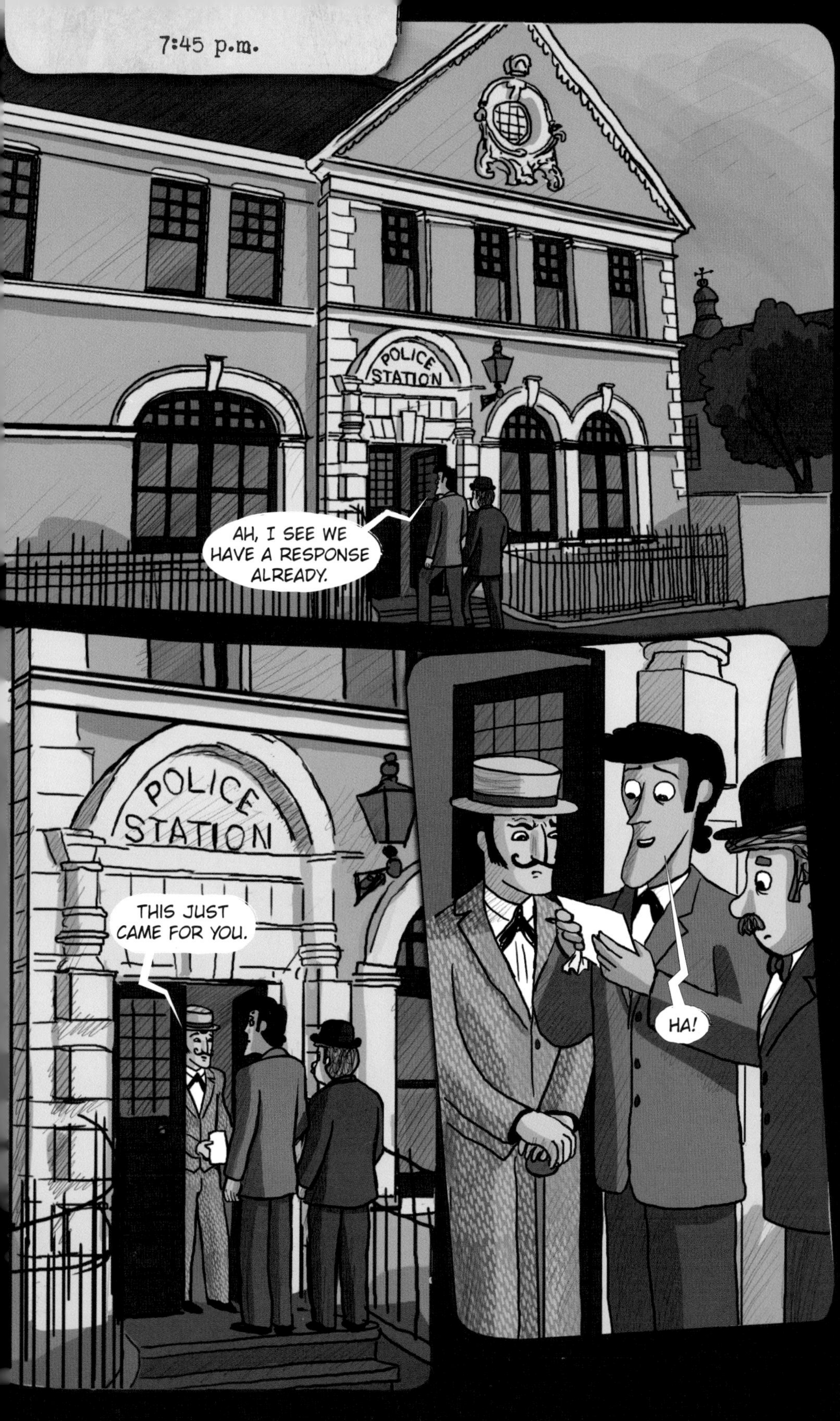
7:45 p.m.
POLICE STATION
AH, I SEE WE HAVE A RESPONSE ALREADY.
POLICE STATION
THIS JUST CAME FOR YOU.
HA!

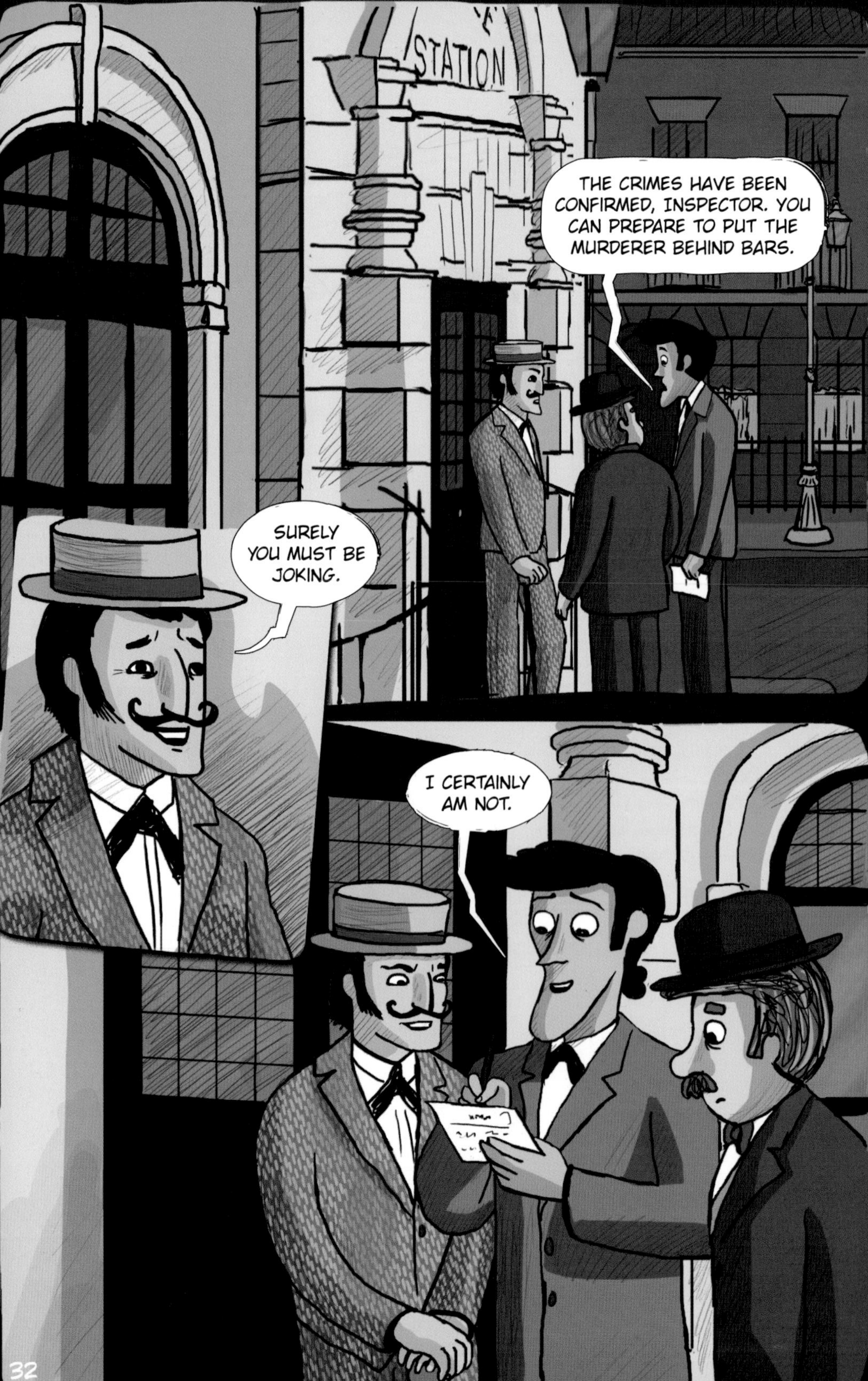
STATION
THE CRIMES HAVE BEEN CONFIRMED, INSPECTOR. YOU CAN PREPARE TO PUT THE MURDERER BEHIND BARS.
SURELY YOU MUST BE JOKING.
I CERTAINLY AM NOT.

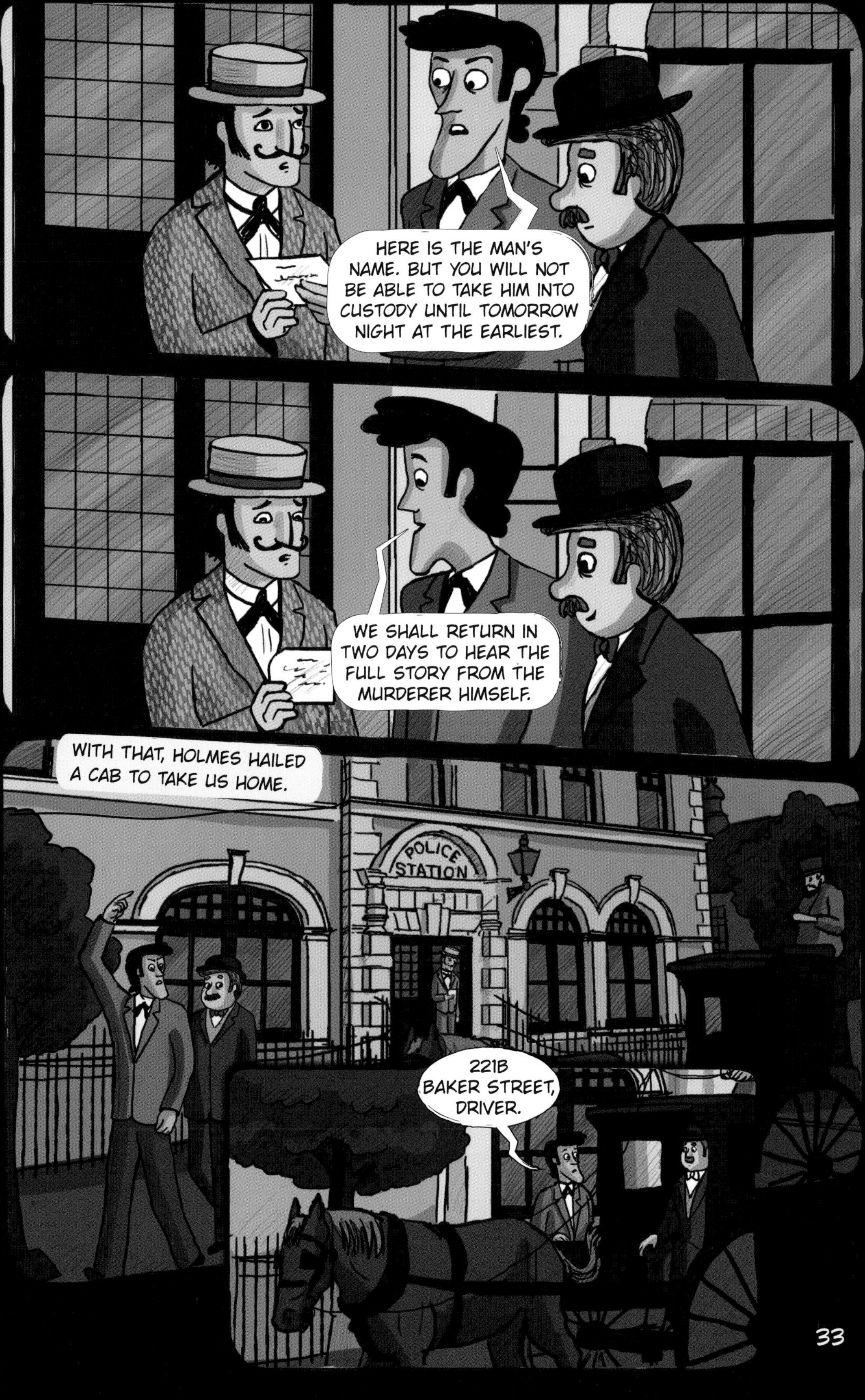
HERE IS THE MAN'S NAME. BUT YOU WILL NOT BE ABLE TO TAKE HIM INTO CUSTODY UNTIL TOMORROW NIGHT AT THE EARLIEST.
WE SHALL RETURN IN TWO DAYS TO HEAR THE FULL STORY FROM THE MURDERER HIMSELF.
WITH THAT, HOLMES HAILED A CAB TO TAKE US HOME.
POLICE STATION
221B BAKER STREET, DRIVER.

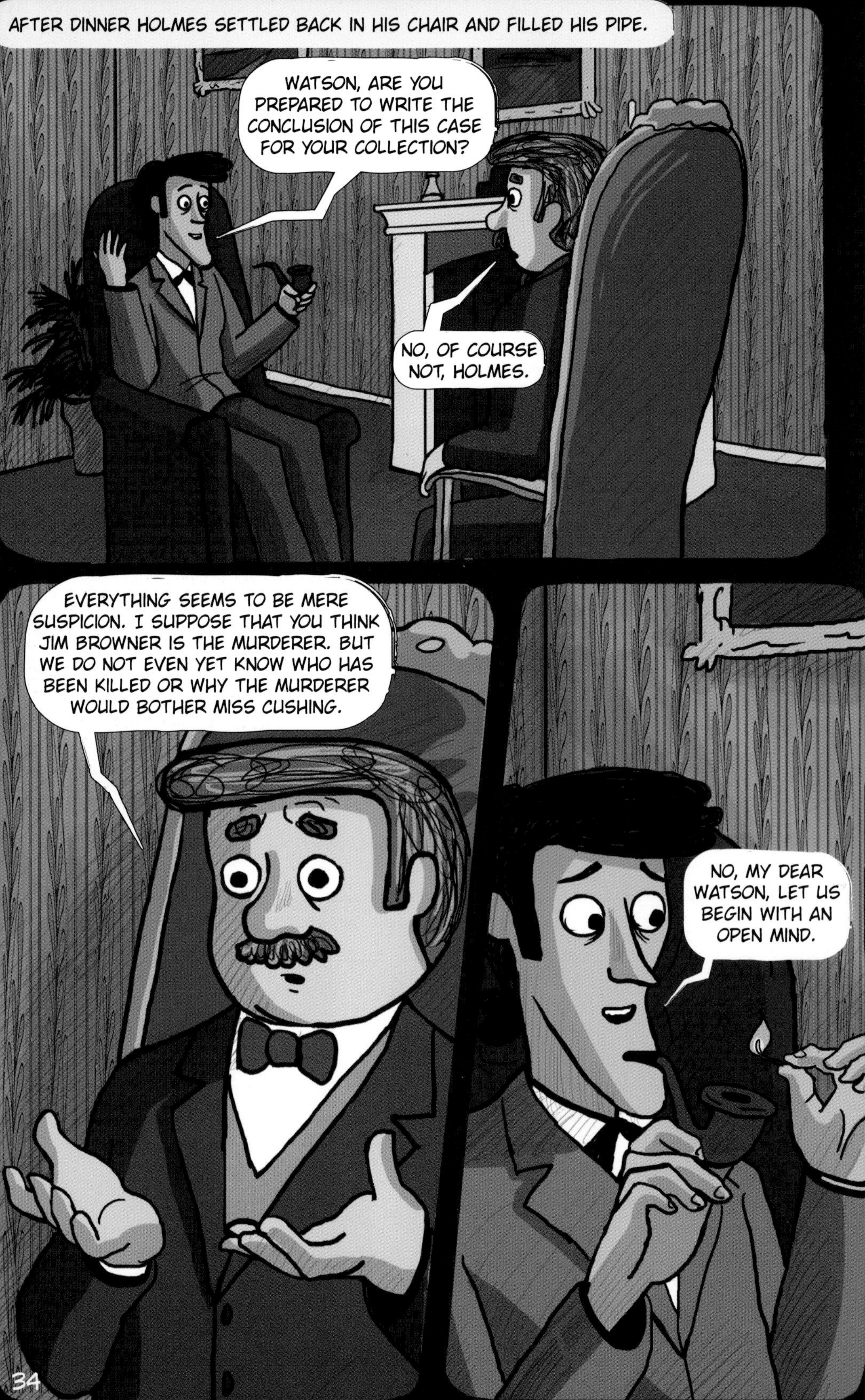
AFTER DINNER HOLMES SETTLED BACK IN HIS CHAIR AND FILLED HIS PIPE.
WATSON, ARE YOU PREPARED TO WRITE THE CONCLUSION OF THIS CASE FOR YOUR COLLECTION?
NO, OF COURSE NOT, HOLMES.
EVERYTHING SEEMS TO BE MERE SUSPICION. I SUPPOSE THAT YOU THINK JIM BROWNER IS THE MURDERER. BUT WE DO NOT EVEN YET KNOW WHO HAS BEEN KILLED OR WHY THE MURDERER WOULD BOTHER MISS CUSHING.
NO, MY DEAR WATSON, LET US BEGIN WITH AN OPEN MIND.

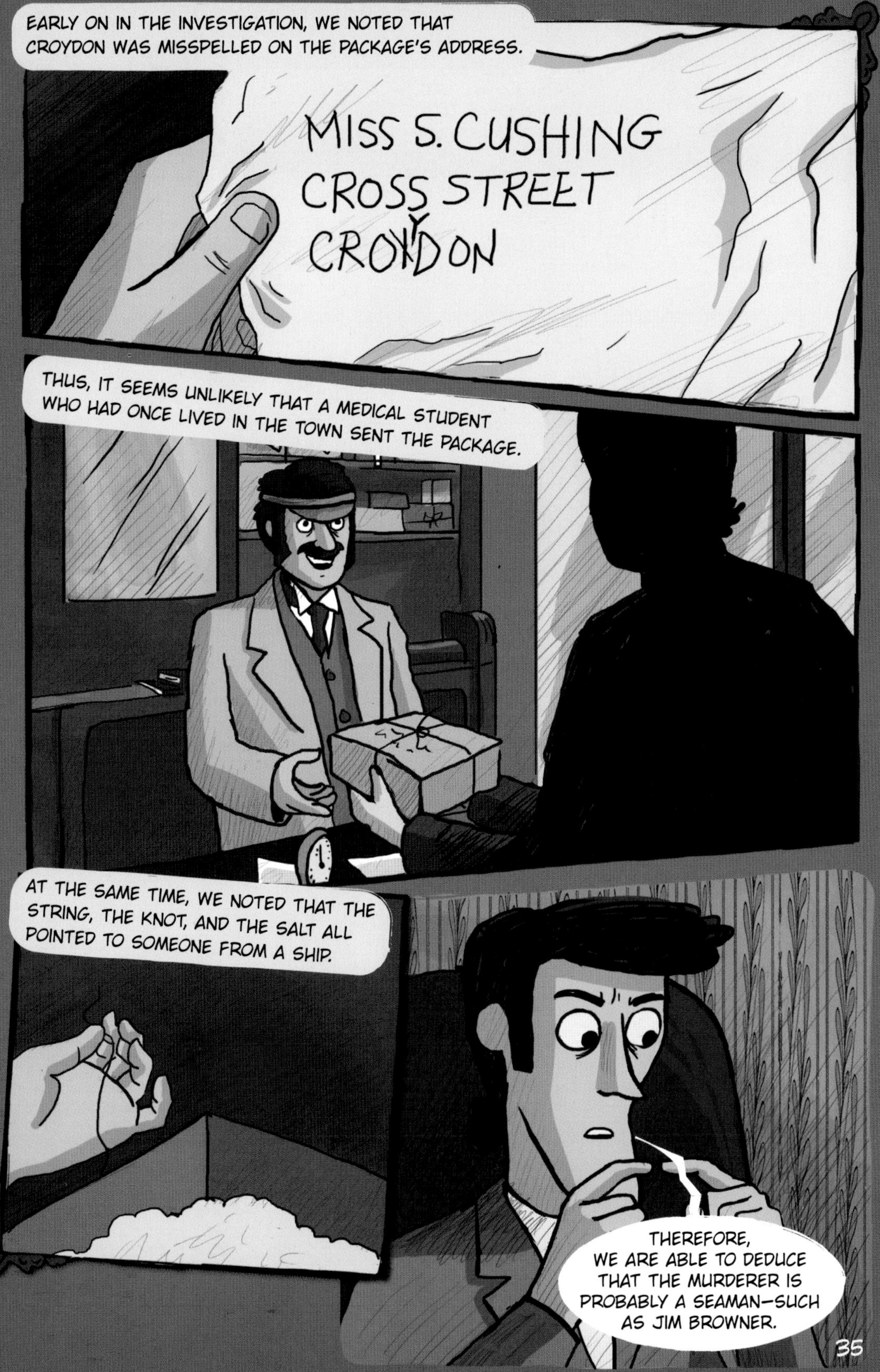
EARLY ON IN THE INVESTIGATION, WE NOTED THAT CROYDON WAS MISSPELLED ON THE PACKAGE'S ADDRESS.
MISS S. CUSHING
CROSS STREET
CROYDON
THUS, IT SEEMS UNLIKELY THAT A MEDICAL STUDENT WHO HAD ONCE LIVED IN THE TOWN SENT THE PACKAGE.
AT THE SAME TIME, WE NOTED THAT THE STRING, THE KNOT, AND THE SALT ALL POINTED TO SOMEONE FROM A SHIP.
THEREFORE, WE ARE ABLE TO DEDUCE THAT THE MURDERER IS PROBABLY A SEAMAN—SUCH AS JIM BROWNER.

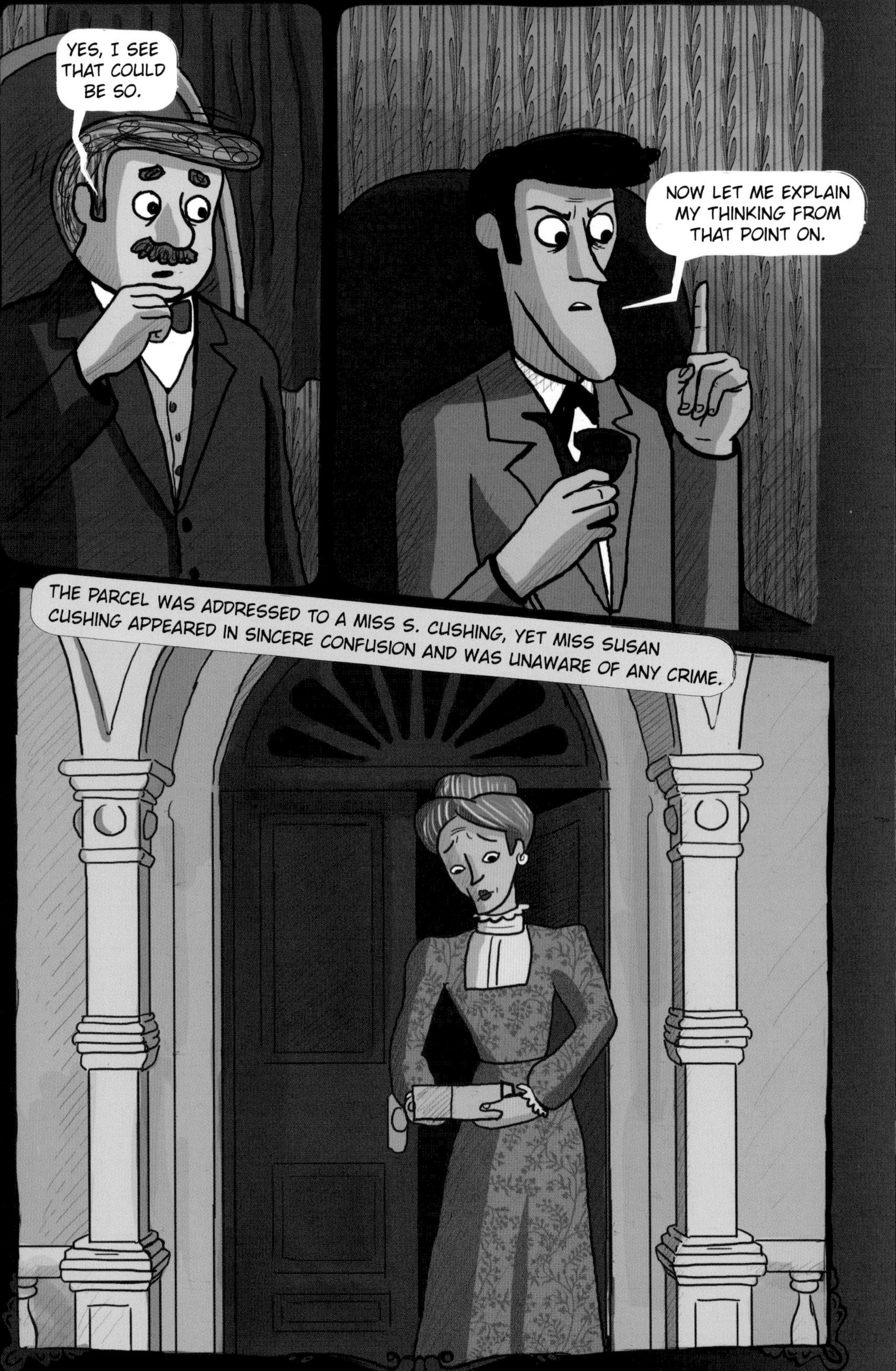
YES, I SEE THAT COULD BE SO.
NOW LET ME EXPLAIN MY THINKING FROM THAT POINT ON.
THE PARCEL WAS ADDRESSED TO A MISS S. CUSHING, YET MISS SUSAN CUSHING APPEARED IN SINCERE CONFUSION AND WAS UNAWARE OF ANY CRIME.

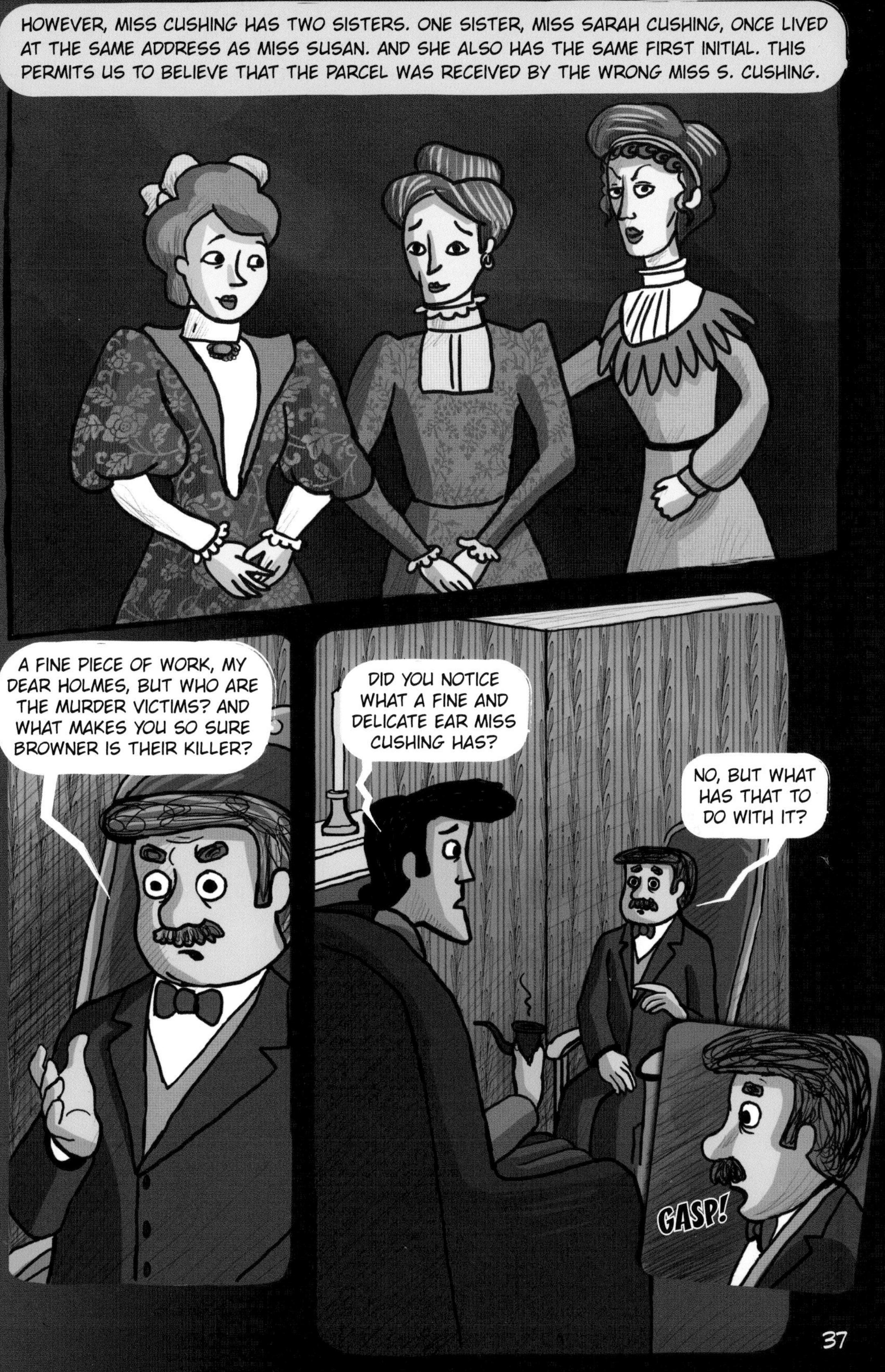
HOWEVER, MISS CUSHING HAS TWO SISTERS. ONE SISTER, MISS SARAH CUSHING, ONCE LIVED AT THE SAME ADDRESS AS MISS SUSAN. AND SHE ALSO HAS THE SAME FIRST INITIAL. THIS PERMITS US TO BELIEVE THAT THE PARCEL WAS RECEIVED BY THE WRONG MISS S. CUSHING.
A FINE PIECE OF WORK, MY DEAR HOLMES, BUT WHO ARE THE MURDER VICTIMS? AND WHAT MAKES YOU SO SURE BROWNER IS THEIR KILLER?
DID YOU NOTICE WHAT A FINE AND DELICATE EAR MISS CUSHING HAS?
NO, BUT WHAT HAS THAT TO DO WITH IT?
GASP!

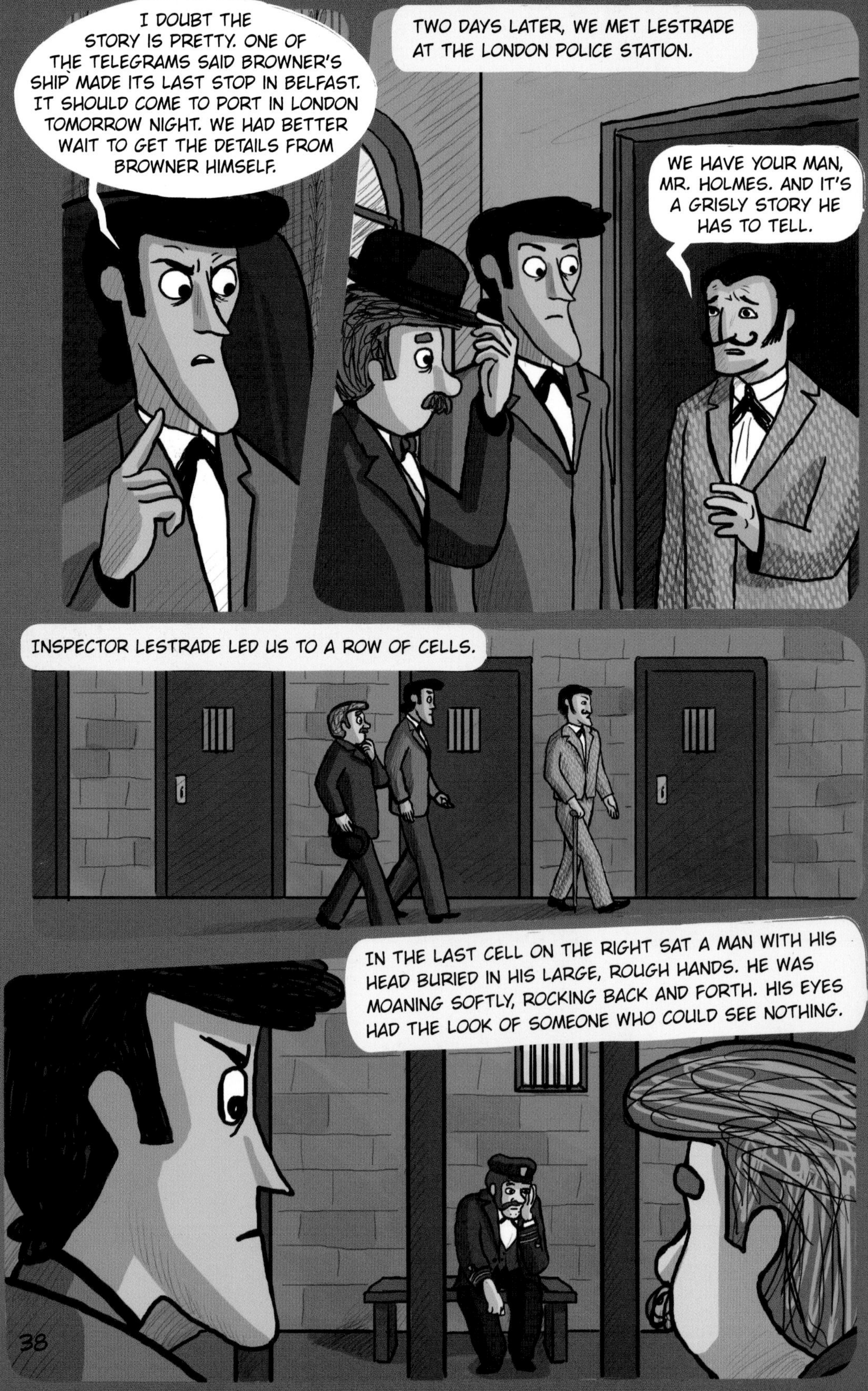
I DOUBT THE STORY IS PRETTY. ONE OF THE TELEGRAMS SAID BROWNER'S SHIP MADE ITS LAST STOP IN BELFAST. IT SHOULD COME TO PORT IN LONDON TOMORROW NIGHT. WE HAD BETTER WAIT TO GET THE DETAILS FROM BROWNER HIMSELF.
TWO DAYS LATER, WE MET LESTRADE AT THE LONDON POLICE STATION.
WE HAVE YOUR MAN, MR. HOLMES. AND IT'S A GRISLY STORY HE HAS TO TELL.
INSPECTOR LESTRADE LED US TO A ROW OF CELLS.
IN THE LAST CELL ON THE RIGHT SAT A MAN WITH HIS HEAD BURIED IN HIS LARGE, ROUGH HANDS. HE WAS MOANING SOFTLY, ROCKING BACK AND FORTH. HIS EYES HAD THE LOOK OF SOMEONE WHO COULD SEE NOTHING.

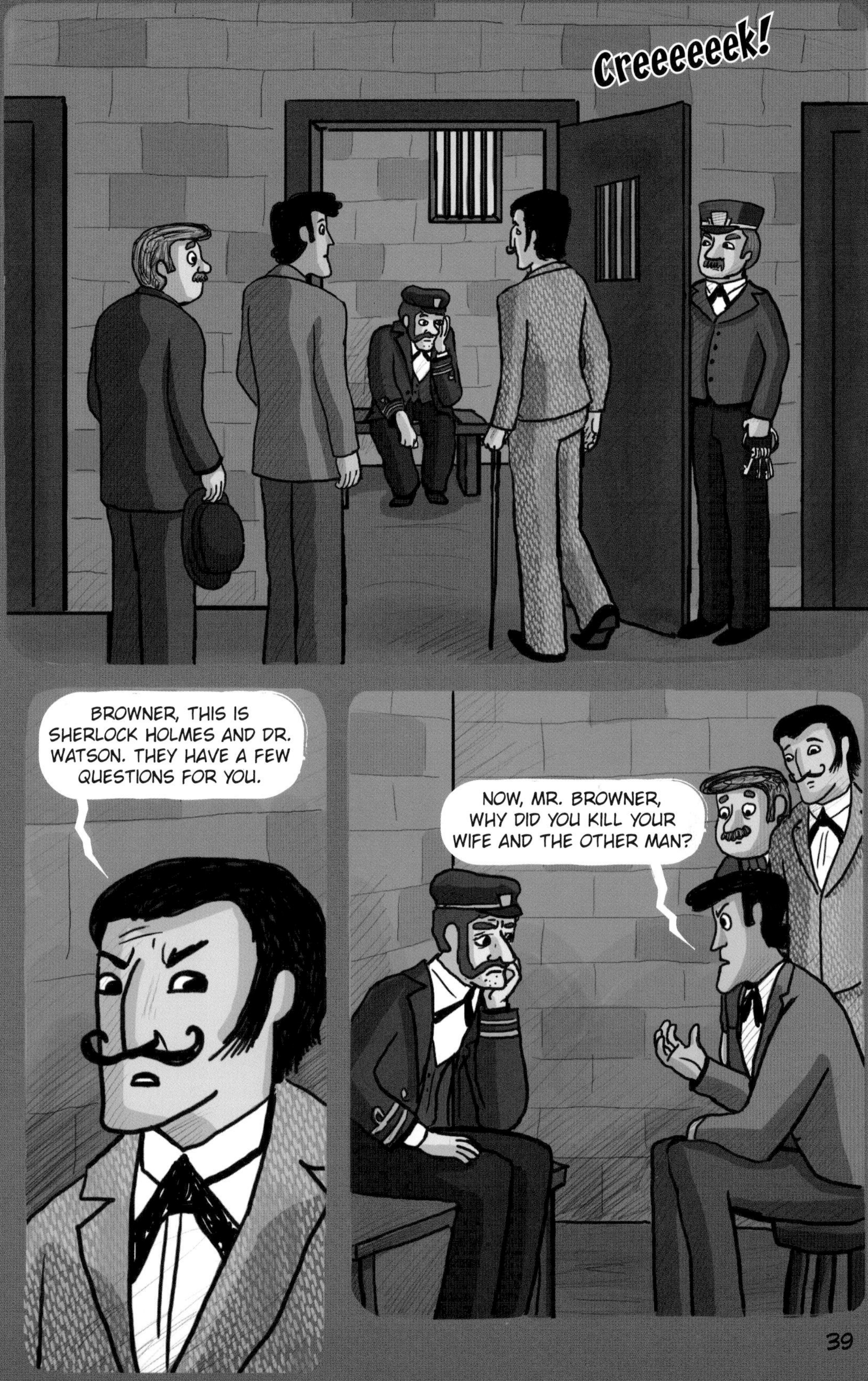
Creeeeeek!
BROWNER, THIS IS SHERLOCK HOLMES AND DR. WATSON. THEY HAVE A FEW QUESTIONS FOR YOU.
NOW, MR. BROWNER, WHY DID YOU KILL YOUR WIFE AND THE OTHER MAN?

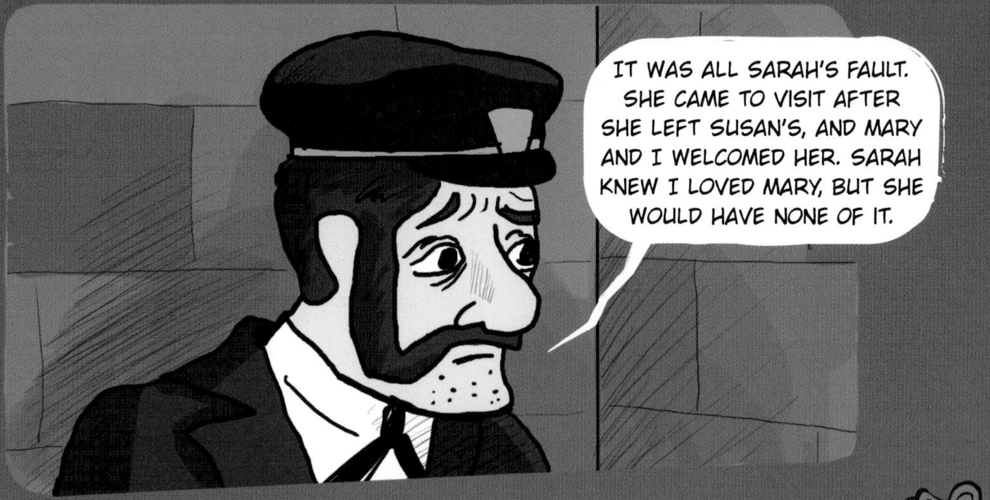
IT WAS ALL SARAH'S FAULT. SHE CAME TO VISIT AFTER SHE LEFT SUSAN'S, AND MARY AND I WELCOMED HER. SARAH KNEW I LOVED MARY, BUT SHE WOULD HAVE NONE OF IT.

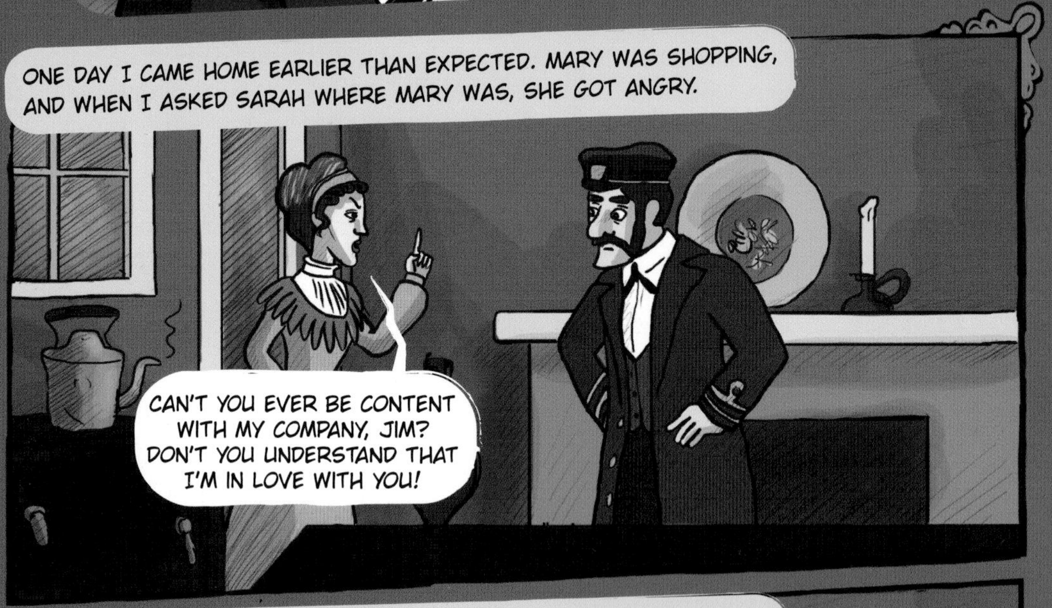
ONE DAY I CAME HOME EARLIER THAN EXPECTED. MARY WAS SHOPPING, AND WHEN I ASKED SARAH WHERE MARY WAS, SHE GOT ANGRY.
CAN'T YOU EVER BE CONTENT WITH MY COMPANY, JIM? DON'T YOU UNDERSTAND THAT I'M IN LOVE WITH YOU!

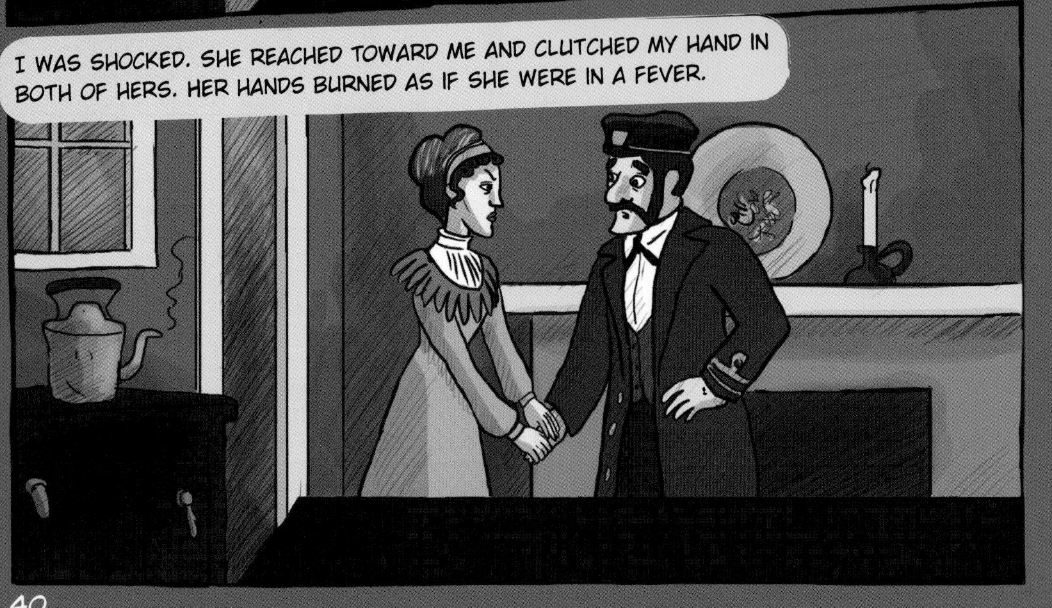
I WAS SHOCKED. SHE REACHED TOWARD ME AND CLUTCHED MY HAND IN BOTH OF HERS. HER HANDS BURNED AS IF SHE WERE IN A FEVER.

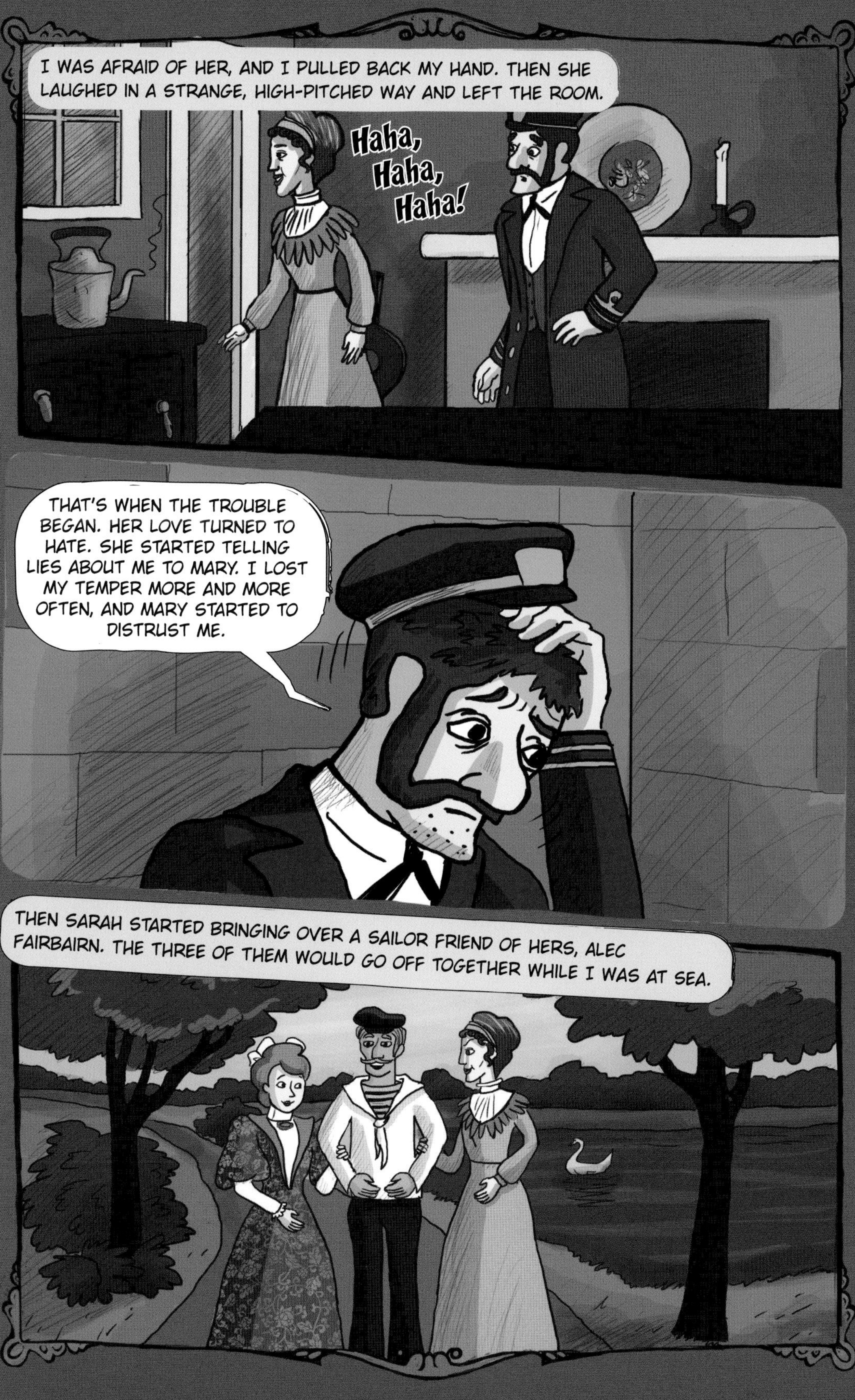
I WAS AFRAID OF HER, AND I PULLED BACK MY HAND. THEN SHE LAUGHED IN A STRANGE, HIGH-PITCHED WAY AND LEFT THE ROOM.
Haha, Haha, Haha!
THAT'S WHEN THE TROUBLE BEGAN. HER LOVE TURNED TO HATE. SHE STARTED TELLING LIES ABOUT ME TO MARY. I LOST MY TEMPER MORE AND MORE OFTEN, AND MARY STARTED TO DISTRUST ME.
THEN SARAH STARTED BRINGING OVER A SAILOR FRIEND OF HERS, ALEC FAIRBAIRN. THE THREE OF THEM WOULD GO OFF TOGETHER WHILE I WAS AT SEA.

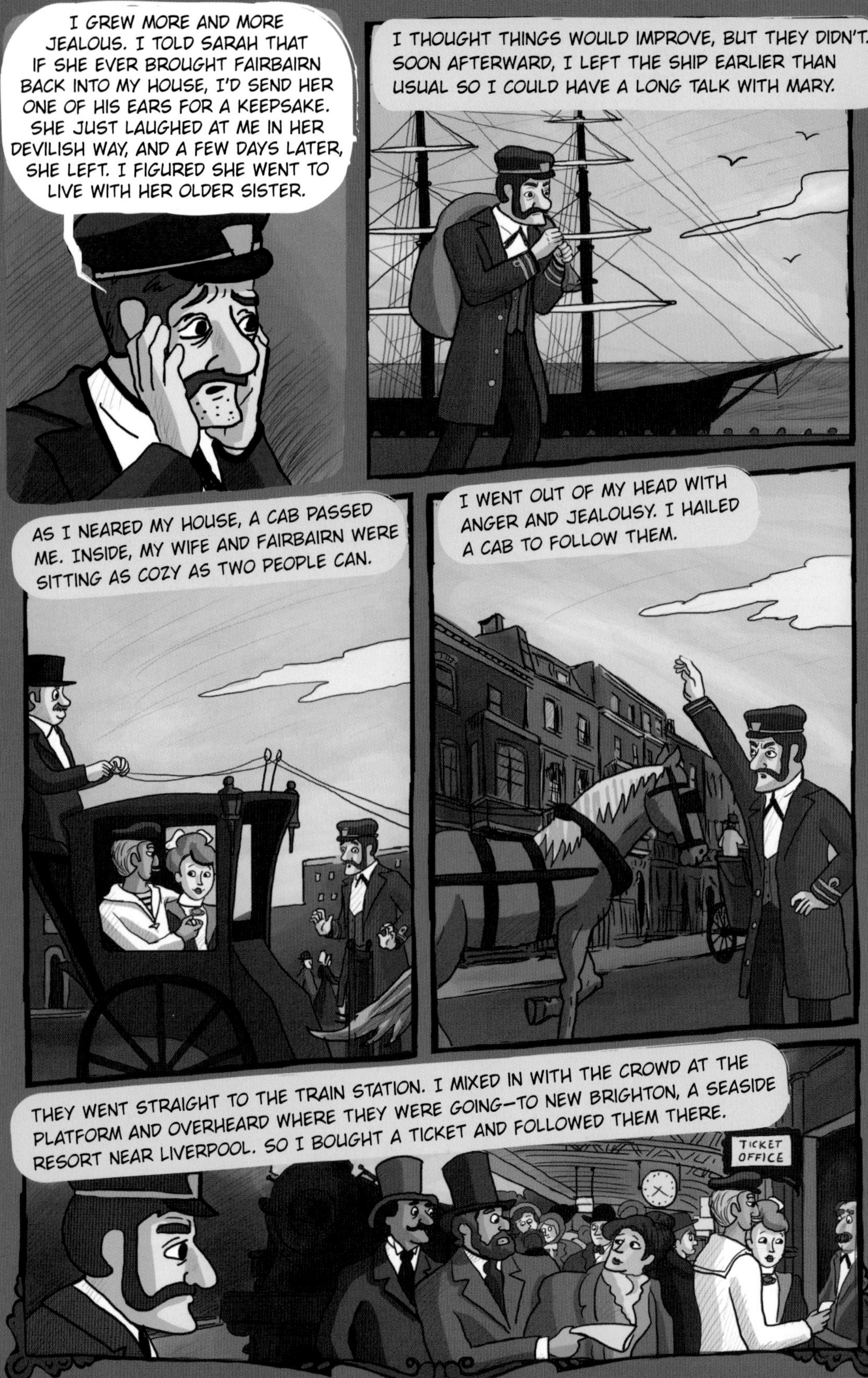
I GREW MORE AND MORE JEALOUS. I TOLD SARAH THAT IF SHE EVER BROUGHT FAIRBAIRN BACK INTO MY HOUSE, I'D SEND HER ONE OF HIS EARS FOR A KEEPSAKE. SHE JUST LAUGHED AT ME IN HER DEVILISH WAY, AND A FEW DAYS LATER, SHE LEFT. I FIGURED SHE WENT TO LIVE WITH HER OLDER SISTER.
I THOUGHT THINGS WOULD IMPROVE, BUT THEY DIDN'T. SOON AFTERWARD, I LEFT THE SHIP EARLIER THAN USUAL SO I COULD HAVE A LONG TALK WITH MARY.
AS I NEARED MY HOUSE, A CAB PASSED ME. INSIDE, MY WIFE AND FAIRBAIRN WERE SITTING AS COZY AS TWO PEOPLE CAN.
I WENT OUT OF MY HEAD WITH ANGER AND JEALOUSY. I HAILED A CAB TO FOLLOW THEM.
THEY WENT STRAIGHT TO THE TRAIN STATION. I MIXED IN WITH THE CROWD AT THE PLATFORM AND OVERHEARD WHERE THEY WERE GOING—TO NEW BRIGHTON, A SEASIDE RESORT NEAR LIVERPOOL. SO I BOUGHT A TICKET AND FOLLOWED THEM THERE.
TICKET OFFICE

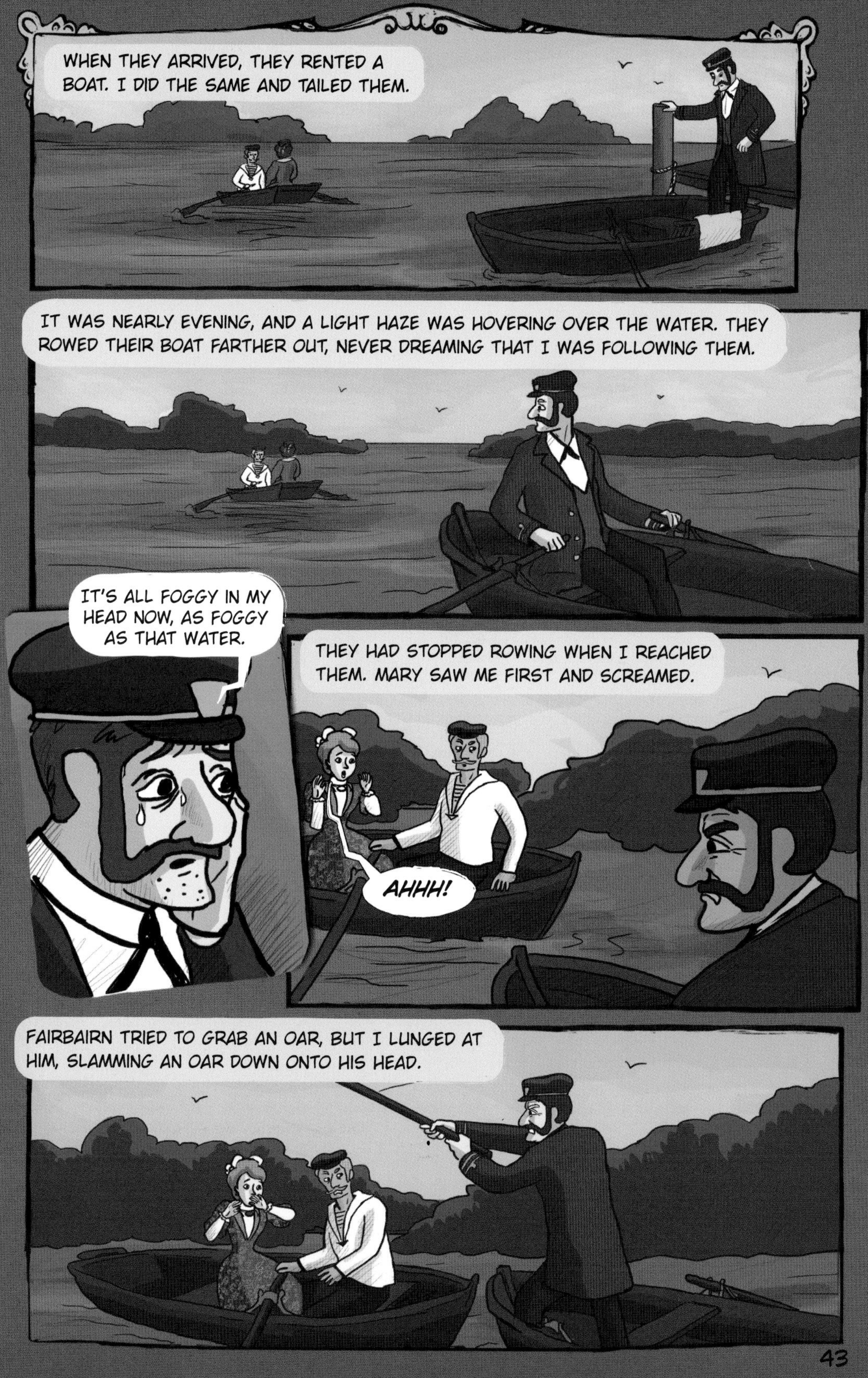
WHEN THEY ARRIVED, THEY RENTED A BOAT. I DID THE SAME AND TAILED THEM.
IT WAS NEARLY EVENING, AND A LIGHT HAZE WAS HOVERING OVER THE WATER. THEY ROWED THEIR BOAT FARTHER OUT, NEVER DREAMING THAT I WAS FOLLOWING THEM.
IT'S ALL FOGGY IN MY HEAD NOW, AS FOGGY AS THAT WATER.
THEY HAD STOPPED ROWING WHEN I REACHED THEM. MARY SAW ME FIRST AND SCREAMED.
AHHH!
FAIRBAIRN TRIED TO GRAB AN OAR, BUT I LUNGED AT HIM, SLAMMING AN OAR DOWN ONTO HIS HEAD.

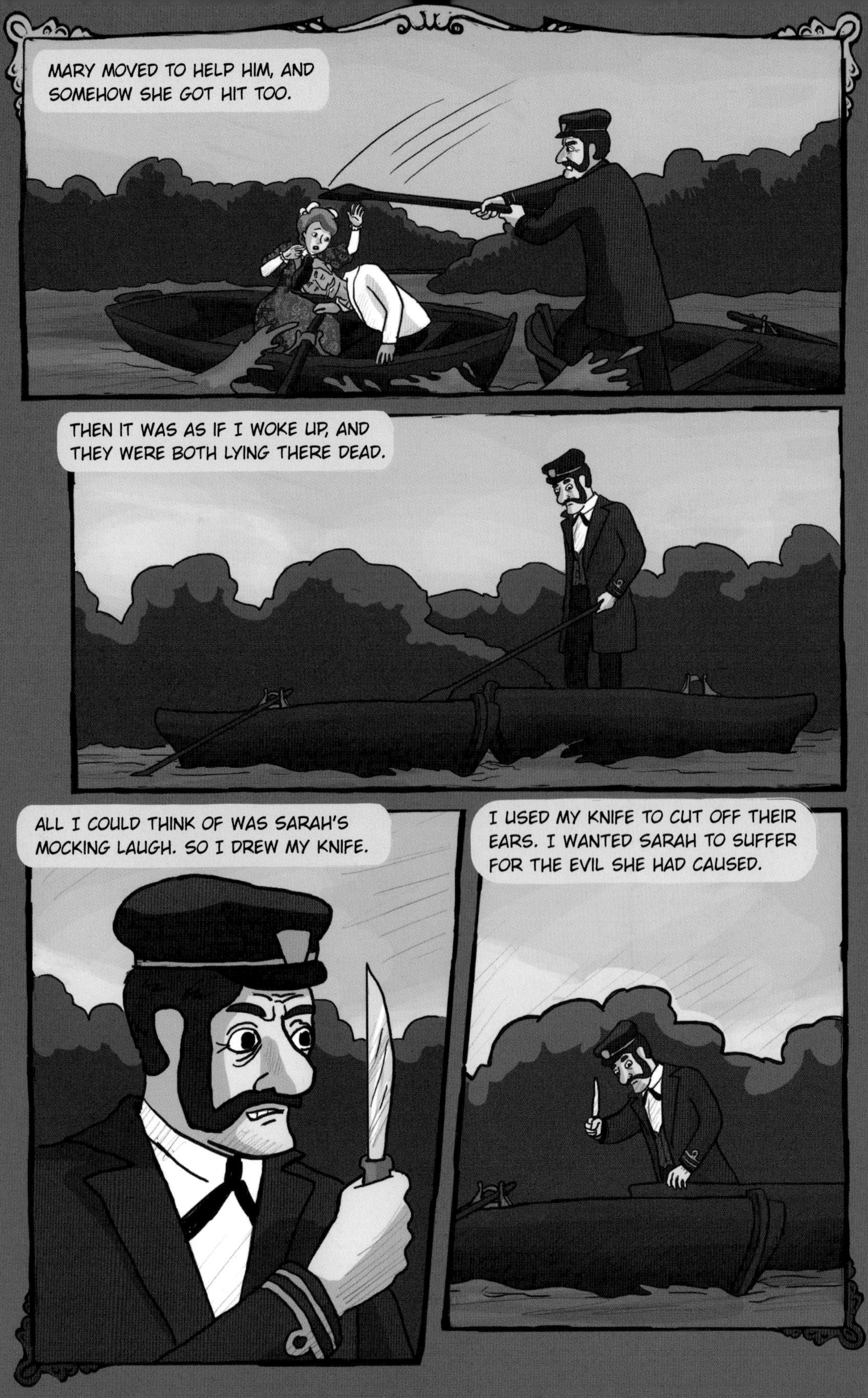
MARY MOVED TO HELP HIM, AND SOMEHOW SHE GOT HIT TOO.
THEN IT WAS AS IF I WOKE UP, AND THEY WERE BOTH LYING THERE DEAD.
ALL I COULD THINK OF WAS SARAH'S MOCKING LAUGH. SO I DREW MY KNIFE.
I USED MY KNIFE TO CUT OFF THEIR EARS. I WANTED SARAH TO SUFFER FOR THE EVIL SHE HAD CAUSED.

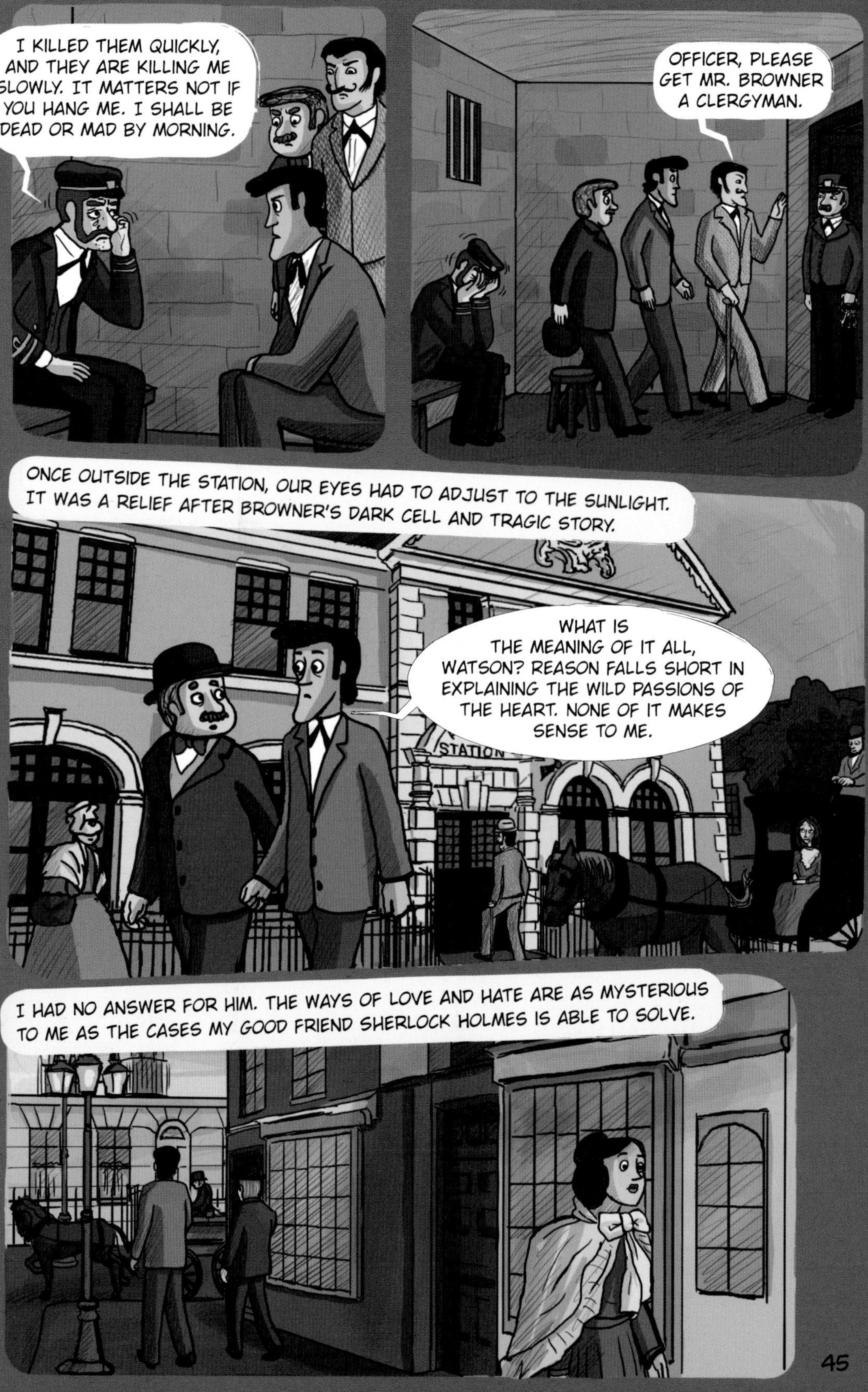

I KILLED THEM QUICKLY, AND THEY ARE KILLING ME SLOWLY. IT MATTERS NOT IF YOU HANG ME. I SHALL BE DEAD OR MAD BY MORNING.
OFFICER, PLEASE GET MR. BROWNER A CLERGYMAN.
ONCE OUTSIDE THE STATION, OUR EYES HAD TO ADJUST TO THE SUNLIGHT. IT WAS A RELIEF AFTER BROWNER'S DARK CELL AND TRAGIC STORY.
WHAT IS THE MEANING OF IT ALL, WATSON? REASON FALLS SHORT IN EXPLAINING THE WILD PASSIONS OF THE HEART. NONE OF IT MAKES SENSE TO ME.
STATION
I HAD NO ANSWER FOR HIM. THE WAYS OF LOVE AND HATE ARE AS MYSTERIOUS TO ME AS THE CASES MY GOOD FRIEND SHERLOCK HOLMES IS ABLE TO SOLVE.

From the Desk of
John H. Watson, M.D.

The Adventure of the Cardboard Box: How Did Holmes Solve It?

How did Holmes narrow the list of possible victims?

When Holmes saw Miss Cushing's profile, he noticed that her ear was very much like the one he had seen in the box. Then he saw the picture of the sisters. Because of the striking resemblances among the three women, he felt certain that the ear in the box belonged to Mary or Sarah.

To confirm that Sarah was not the sister murdered, Holmes went to visit her. He discovered that she was alive but very ill. He concluded that Sarah had read the newspaper account and knew who had been murdered and why. Her guilt and horror had made her ill.

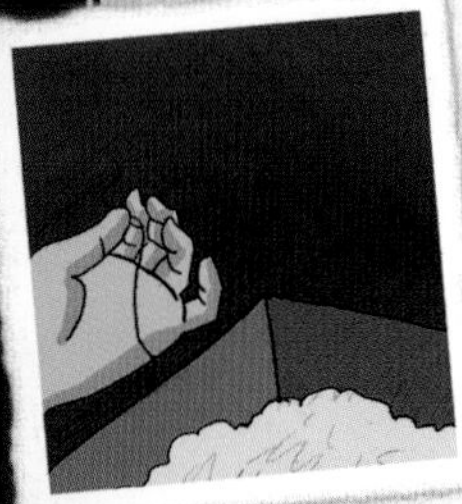

Knowing Sarah was alive, Holmes deduced that Mary must be dead. To check this, he wired the Liverpool police to see if she was at home. They telegraphed back that there had been no answer at her house for the past three days. Holmes was sure then that Mary had been murdered.

How did Holmes determine the suspect?

The twine and salt from the box indicated someone familiar with the sea. When Holmes discovered that Miss Cushing had a brother-in-law who worked on an England-Ireland shipping line, he suspected Browner was involved.

How was Holmes able to conclude that Browner committed the murders?

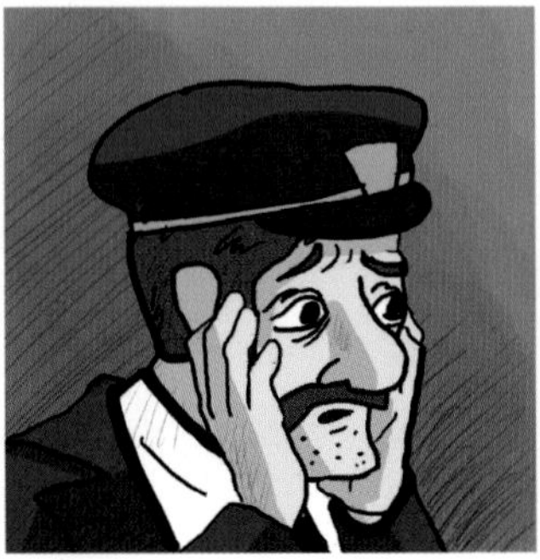

Holmes could not conclude if Browner was the murderer or the man murdered. So Holmes wired the shipping line to find out whether Browner had reported for work and if the ship had stopped in Belfast. When the shipping company telegraphed back that Browner was at work and that the ship had stopped at Belfast on Thursday, Holmes knew Browner was the murderer.

How was Holmes able to confirm who the other victim was?

One mystery still remained: Who was the man killed? Holmes suspected the man was a sailor because his ear was sunburned and pierced for an earring. But only Browner and Sarah knew the man's name and exactly why he had been killed.

Further Reading and Websites

The Beacon Society
http://beaconsociety.com/Student.html

Dowd, Siobhan. *The London Eye Mystery.* New York: Random House, 2007.

Hautman, Peter. *Snatched.* New York: Penguin Group, 2006.

MysteryNet.com CSI: Crime Scene Investigation
http://www.mysterynet.com/tv/profiles/csi-crime-scene-investigation/

Poe, Edgar Allen, and Gris Grimly. *Tales of Mystery and Madness.* New York: Atheneum, 2004.

Sherlock Holmes Museum
http://www.sherlock-holmes.co.uk

Springer, Nancy. *The Case of the Missing Marquess.* New York: Penguin Group, 2006.

Summy, Barbara. *I So Don't Do Mysteries.* New York: Random House, 2008.

221 Baker Street
http://221bakerstreet.org

Yoder, Eric. *One Minute Mysteries: 65 Short Mysteries You Solve With Science.* Washington, DC: Science Naturally, 2008.

About the Author

Sir Arthur Conan Doyle was born on May 22, 1859. He became a doctor in 1882. When this career did not prove successful, Doyle started writing stories. In addition to the popular Sherlock Holmes short stories and novels, Doyle also wrote historical novels, romances, and plays.

About the Adapters

Murray Shaw's lifelong passion for Sherlock Holmes began when he was a child. He was the author of the Match Wits with Sherlock Holmes series published in the 1990s. For decades, he was a popular speaker in public schools and libraries on the adventures of Holmes and Watson.

M. J. Cosson is the author of more than fifty books, both fiction and nonfiction, for children and young adults. She has long been a fan of mysteries and especially of the great detective, Sherlock Holmes. In fact, she has participated in the production of several Sherlock Holmes plays. A native of Iowa, Cosson lives in the Texas Hill Country with her husband, dogs, and cat.

About the Illustrators

Sophie Rohrbach began her career after graduating in display design at the Chambre des Commerce in France. She went on to design displays in many top department stores including Galerias Lafayette. She also studied illustration at Emile Cohl school in Lyon, France, where she now lives with her daughter. Rohrbach has illustrated many children's books. She is passionate about the colors and patterns that she uses in her illustrations.

JT Morrow has worked as a freelance illustrator for over twenty years and has won several awards. He specializes in doing parodies and imitations of the Old and Modern Masters—everyone from da Vinci to Picasso. JT also exhibits his paintings at galleries near his home. He lives just south of San Francisco with his wife and daughter.